My Life as the Ugly Stepsister
(A Young Adult Romance)

Juli Alexander

ISBN-10:1475280513

ISBN-13:978-1475280517

DEDICATION

For every girl who thinks she isn't the prettiest one in the room..

ACKNOWLEDGMENTS

Thanks to SMRW, my friends, my family, and my critique group. .

CHAPTER ONE

Do not teach your mother to use the Internet. No good can come of it. -Ally's Brutal Teen Truths

"What do you mean we may be moving to Seattle to live with your Internet boyfriend? That's insane." I glared at my mother over the half-empty pizza box. "It's all the way across the country."

I swear it will be a miracle if I make it through my teens without a psychiatric hospitalization. I forgot to breathe for a moment. Oh my God, I started high school in less than two weeks and she wanted to move?

My mom tried to smile, but even she knew this was not the time. "Calm down, Ally. Let me explain."

I don't know about you, but when people tell me to calm down, it makes me really, really want to smack them.

"You aren't coming with me." She lifted her paper plate and stacked it on top of mine. Mom worked long hours and doing dishes was the one thing she'd cut out for New Year's. She'd cut out home-cooked meals when Dad left two years ago.

"What!" Even worse than uprooting me, she was totally abandoning me? Then I realized the horrible truth. "I am not living with Dad and Diane. No way." Dread unfurled in my stomach.

Mojo, my black and tan hound, came into the kitchen to check on the ruckus. He gave Mom a curious look and slipped under the table to lie at my feet.

Mom put on her "Let's be reasonable" face. "Now, Ally. It's just for four months. That's it. It's like summer vacation. It will be over before you know it."

I hadn't seen this coming. Not at all. All those hours Mom spent on the phone with that guy in Seattle. I'd thought it was harmless. I'd actually believed it was good for her. "Mom, I'm sure you can find somebody here in Charlotte to date. You're not ugly or anything."

She flinched but obviously decided to ignore my insulting compliment. "I think Donald may be my Mr. Right. I'd really like to give this relationship a chance, but long distance just isn't practical. I don't want to uproot you without knowing for sure." She ran her hand through the fresh red highlights in her brown hair. Her natural color hadn't been good enough since the divorce.

"Why can't he just come here?" I was barely coping with the known, no way could I handle the unknown. "What's so great about Seattle?"

"Donald's worked hard to build his insurance business, Ally. He can't just leave it. But there is always work for an experienced paralegal. I've already got two job offers. Besides, he's got an apartment over the garage."

My stomach cramped at the betrayal. She'd applied for jobs before talking to me.

Mom pressed on, "Besides, if things work out between Donald and me, I know you'd be happy there. Seattle is supposed to be beautiful. The Emerald City with evergreen trees and mountains. They say it's just spectacular."

"We have trees and mountains around here. People move to North Carolina all the time for the *spectacular*," I mimicked Mom's emphasis on the word, "views."

"You could learn to ski."

"I can ski here. In North Carolina." I crossed my arms. "Where we live now."

"You'll be right on the Pacific coast."

"We can drive to the Atlantic anytime we want." I accidentally applied too much tension and snapped my plastic fork in half, sticking my finger. "Ow." No blood at least. Wait a minute. Back up. She was living over his garage. Right.

"Ally, I know you're upset," she said, ignoring my cry of pain. "That's why I'm asking you to stay with your dad for four months. Let me see if this relationship is worth it."

I looked into the green eyes of the woman who'd raised me, hating her calm expression. "So you'll forget the whole thing in four months if you don't like him?"

"Yes." Her shoulders relaxed a little. "I just want to give it a chance."

"Okay. So if your relationship with this guy is like a four on a scale of one to ten, you'll come home?"

"Yes."

"What if it's a six?"

"Probably." She shrugged. "Ally, I really can't give you any probabilities. Love is not a science."

Love. Barf! This was all Dad's fault for leaving Mom in the first place. Now she was dating, shaving her legs regularly, coloring her hair, and leaving me.

"You know I can't stand Diane! I would never, ever make you live in the same house with her."

Mom pressed her lips together for a moment. Then, she said in a maddeningly calm voice, "It's not exactly the same situation. I won't say she's one of my favorite people, but four months with her will not kill you." She stood and took the dishes to the garbage can.

I could think of a whole lot of things my mother had said about Diane. And a lot of them involved words she'd punish me for saying. Somehow I kept from mentioning those tirades. The reminder would only trigger one of those therapist-induced-apology-slash-lectures I'd heard too many times lately.

Mom had spent most of the last two years in therapy. She'd progressed from crying most of the day to behaving somewhat like a normal person. Unfortunately, her total immersion in Dr. Phil and friends had not managed to make my quality of life any better. I mean, at least she cried on the couch in our house in Charlotte. Not two thousand freaking miles away. Okay, I knew I'd feel guilty about wishing her back to the crying stage, but right now, I was totally entitled to be obnoxious. The woman was wrecking my life, and it wasn't that great anyway.

She walked back to the table and sat down. "Ally, Seattle is supposed to be a really cool place for young people. That's where Starbucks and those grunge bands started. The birthplace of Nirvana?"

Oh, come on! "The lead singer was an addict who shot himself in the head. If that's your example of a good reason to move, you've got serious parenting deficits." I stopped short of asking what Dr. Phil would say. Even my mother had limits.

"I'm sorry to disrupt your life, but—"

And that's when I tuned out, because that's the beginning of the speech I've heard a hundred times before about how my mother can't keep putting herself last. I nodded and uh-huhed at all the right spots while I tried to wrap my mind around the chaos that had taken over my life.

One, my mom was moving to Seattle.

Which meant, two that I'd have to live with my dad.

Who, three lived with the home-wrecking hag he'd married.

Who, four had a daughter my age who was ridiculously beautiful.

Which meant, five that I was living the next four months as the ugly stepsister.

On the bright side, my self-esteem wasn't all that high anyway, so this experience should serve well to bottom it out. And once I was a total wreck, psycho, blubbering idiot, it would finally be my turn for my needs to come first. Because in my family, the one closest to the ledge got to make the choices.

Mom definitely looked like a woman on the edge. She had finally stopped lecturing, and she had her hand on her throat like she does when she's about to throw up. She didn't deal with stress very well, and she obviously felt bad about the whole thing. But that hadn't stopped her. If I didn't think fast, she'd be on a plane to Seattle, and I'd be living with the stepmonster.

Unless... "Dad and Diane probably won't want me to live there. They don't have a very big house. And Dad is gone so much. Diane won't go along with this."

Her hands flew to her hips and she harrumphed. "I knew you weren't listening, Ally. I just told you that they're looking forward to it. Your father thinks it's a great way for you to get to know Diane better."

Well, there goes that theory. The anger finally bubbled over. "Is there anyone who doesn't know about this before I do?" I shouted. "Have you talked to everyone but me?"

"Ally, I had to make arrangements. I'm leaving in two weeks. It couldn't all wait until the last minute—"

"I don't want to hear it," I said, jumping up and leaving the kitchen.

I ran up the stairs, waited for my dog to follow me into my room, slammed my door, locked it, and plopped down on my bed. I was literally seeing red. And it was only partly because my curtains and bedspread were red. Mostly, it was rage. With a little dread and fear thrown in. Luckily for me, the tears washed some of it away. Mojo jumped up and licked at my face, but I finally got him to settle down and lay down beside me. Mojo understood my pain. He was the best dog in the world. I'd found him at the pound three years earlier, and we'd been inseparable ever since.

After I'd soaked my pillow with various bodily fluids (Why does crying make your nose run, anyway?), I rolled over onto my back and called Madison on my candy apple red cell phone.

I folded the pillow in half, damp side down, and shoved it under my neck. "You won't believe this," I said, and I told her what was happening.

"Oh my God," Madison said when I finished.

Her reaction confirmed just how horrible this was. Usually I couldn't get her to shut up. Now she couldn't think of anything to say. There was a really, really long pause. Then she said, "How could she do that to you?"

"I know!" I scratched behind Mojo's ears and looked into his big, brown eyes. Poor homeless mutt. Poor abandoned me.

"Are you sure you aren't being punk'd? I just can't see your mother leaving you, um, I mean leaving here, to live on the other side of the country."

Ouch. Leaving me. I could count on Madison to say it like it was. "Do you really think there's a show where mean mothers make their daughters cry?"

"No." She sounded disappointed as if she was hoping to meet Ashton. "I guess not. But your mom is usually so nice. She lets us sleepover all the time. She seems kind of sad sometimes, but not mean."

Mom was definitely sad. Luckily, I was too angry to feel guilty about it.

"Maybe it will be cool to live with Caroline," Madison said, taking a shot at lifting my spirits.

Madison admired my stepsister Caroline. Everyone did. Even I liked Caroline. I just didn't like myself when I was around her. "I'm sure she'll be just thrilled to have me dumped into her space all of a sudden."

"It's your space too. Your dad lives there."

True, but he lived there because he'd moved away from me and my mom. That little tidbit didn't increase my comfort level. "How about you and me just trade lives for four months?"

Madison laughed. "My life isn't so great either. Even with soccer, my mom won't let me quit choir this year. And you know I can't sing."

She really couldn't. Our school let everybody in the choir. Madison just stood there moving her mouth. The few times she actually tried to sing, people around her thought a sheep was getting strangled. "Can your mom sing?"

"She thinks she can," Madison said. "At Mass it's all I can do not to run screaming for the door."

"You're probably getting double credit for going then. I think I've got enough credits to stop going to Mass until I'm thirty, so God will probably spot you another ten years for your suffering. It's like you've got a bank full of prepaid penance." I looked at Mojo and he panted in agreement.

"Do you think so?"

"I do. And besides, you only have two choir concerts a year."

"I just hate being reminded of how pathetic I am at every practice."

That was kind of why I didn't like being around my stepsister. "You're not pathetic," I assured her. "Now your mother..."

Madison giggled. "I'm going to make you sit with us next time."

"Can't," I said, searching for an excuse. "I have to sit in the back. I've got..." What was that commercial that was always on. Oh yeah. "I've got an overactive bladder."

"Right," she said obviously not buying it. "We can sit in the back too. We aren't picky."

Actually, Madison's mother insisted on sitting near the front of the large cathedral every Sunday. I personally thought she liked to be seen in her expensive clothes. Unlike Madison, her mother was an attention seeker. And she spent big bucks on her wardrobe. My mom thought Elaine was insecure because her husband was a big-time heart surgeon. Lots of the kids at school were doctor's kids, and Madison was the only one who was really cool.

"I'm being punished enough, Madison. Give me a break."

She sighed. "You're probably right."

I added another entry in my journal of Brutal Teen Truths. *Do not teach your mother to use the Internet. No good can come of it.* This joined tidbits of painfully acquired information like: *You will always get a zit when you need to look good,* and *It's very difficult for teens to hire a hit man.*

I'd started out with "One Million Reasons Divorce Sucks," but after two years, it had fallen by the wayside. Just to be thorough, I added a few more to that list. I was up to seven hundred and ten. Then, I spent a few hours on the Internet, trying to distract myself. When it hit me that Mom's new boyfriend probably had a site, I ran a search.

Donald Waller, Independent Insurance Agent. He had a site all right. I clicked the link and music blared from my speakers when the site loaded. It sounded like an action movie soundtrack, but as the intro started, I realized it must be some kind of superhero music. The intro showed a red cartoon car crashing into a blue one. Bam! The word was surrounded by that funny looking balloon, like in a comic book. Then an animated figure in a cape swooped in. His costume proclaimed him to be "Captain Coverage."

The intro ended and a picture came up of Captain Coverage. Only this time, he had a cut-out real picture of his face photo-shopped over the cartoon. Donald Waller was a big-time, fifty-something geek.

The rest of the site looked pretty normal. Like an insurance website should, I guess.

I could probably live through Mom leaving me for four months a lot easier than I could do without her forever. This guy looked scary. Internet dating wasn't safe, was it? And Seattle was forever away. A six-hour plane ride. A four-day drive. Two days by train. Okay, so I'd looked into it.

I shut down my laptop and went in to my mother's room. She was asleep, and the digital clock next to the bed read 12:30.

"Mom," I said, creeping around the oversized furniture in the room.

She jumped and opened her eyes. She'd always been a light sleeper. "What's wrong? Are you sick?"

"No, but I need to talk to you." She didn't look so hot without her makeup.

She blinked. "Okay."

"I just went to Donald's website," I said.

"Yes." She sat up and tugged at the comforter.

"And, um, he doesn't seem entirely normal."

Mom nodded wearily. "You know, Ally. We all have our little quirks. He's a huge comic book fan. He's really a decent guy though."

"What if he's not? What if he's a serial killer and he chops you into bits?"

Mom winced. "He's not, Ally. I don't take my safety lightly. Stacy Barnett was by the office the other day. She's the private investigator the firm uses."

I nodded.

The brown smudges under her eyes added years to her appearance. "I had her do a background check. Everything looks fine."

I crossed my arms. "All that means is that he hasn't murdered anybody yet."

"Right. And that's all he knows about me too. I know it's rough right now, but it will be okay. We may not really hit it off, but he won't hurt me."

Not like my dad did when he cheated on her. She didn't say it, but I knew she was thinking it. "I'm going to bed now."

"Good night, Sweetie. I love you." She held out her arms and I leaned in for a hug. She squeezed extra tight, and for a moment I felt like a well-protected little girl again.

"I love you too," I said and ambled back to my room. Compared to a brutal murder, a short-term abandonment seemed do-able.

CHAPTER TWO

Your parents control your life absolutely and completely and there isn't a darn thing you can do about it.
--Ally's Brutal Teen Truths

Mom wasn't leaving for two weeks, but she insisted I spend the first week with my dad. "Once you get settled in, you'll see it's not as bad as you think."

Yeah. Right. She probably just wanted to put the house up for sale while I wasn't paying attention. Okay, she wouldn't do that after telling me I had four months. She did have some integrity.

Panic gripped my chest as I stalked up the sidewalk rolling my overstuffed suitcase behind me.

Diane's heavily lipsticked lips curved into a smile as she opened the door and told me we were going to have "lots of fun together."

I kept my eyes averted from her chest. She liked to wear low-cut tops for some reason. Personally, I thought it was pretty trashy. And gross.

"It's a shame," she said, as she gave a fake little wave to Mom out by the curb, "that Caroline isn't back yet. She should be home by this afternoon."

"Yeah," I said, lugging my suitcase, my laptop, and purse, past her and up the stairs. The air was heavily scented with air freshener as usual. Diane's paintings covered the foyer walls which rose two stories. She was definitely painting for quantity instead of quality. I think I liked the modern art better than the crudely painted floral arrangements. All in all, I'd much rather her spend her time painting than bugging me.

I couldn't decide if I'd rather have Caroline around or not. She would keep Diane occupied, but I didn't know if my ego could take interaction on a daily basis with someone that beautiful.

Caroline could model, and actually had modeled some in print ads. Dad had thought it was so fortunate that his new wife had a daughter exactly my age. She was actually a week younger. But the sad thing was that when you all the sudden had a drop-dead gorgeous stepsister and you were average looking but not hideous... Even if you were sort of pretty. And by you, I meant me—having Caroline around delegated me to the role of the ugly stepsister. My hair was medium brown and wavy. Hers was dark chocolate and fashionably straight. Her big, almond-shaped eyes made mine appear smaller and sleepier. My face was roundish. She had cheekbones.

And yet I couldn't hate her. She was friendly, confident, and popular. She was nice to me, and she had a brain. I was probably a little bit smarter than her, but she planned to go to law school. She'd do really well. Caroline had two older stepbrothers in Atlanta. Boys did not intimidate her one bit. Of course, guys were less threatening when they were drooling all over themselves and falling at your feet. Not that I'd know for sure, but it seemed preferable to the reaction I got from boys. Which was usually no reaction at all.

I tramped up the stairs, through the cloud of Diane's perfume, straining a little with my burdens. I reached the top and rolled my suitcase down the hall to the room they'd designated as mine when they'd bought the house. Caroline had the bigger room because she lived there full time. But the third bedroom in the split foyer was just fine by me. I'd painted it blue and picked out a bright yellow comforter for the double bed. I wanted to see something cheerful when I first woke up. Not that I spent much time there. There wasn't room for much else in there besides a desk, but the closet was set up pretty well. I saw that Diane had removed the vacuum cleaner and winter jackets since my last visit. The room was fine for weekends, but I didn't look forward to spending four straight months in there.

Dad's house was older than the rancher Mom had gotten in the divorce. I knew Dad didn't like split foyers, but I also knew that he was paying Mom a lot of alimony for the first five years. Apparently, this was all he and Diane could afford. The house was pretty good size, just not brand-spanking new. Since Diane had quit her part-time job the moment they married to pursue her "love for art," she'd set up the living room as a studio. The family room downstairs was where I usually hung out. Dad's television was bigger than my mother's of course, and he had the place wired with surround sound. He had an office in the bedroom downstairs that he used sometimes. Well, it was really more of a computer museum than an office. Dad worked in network installations and traveled a lot. Since Caroline had the most active social life of any fourteen-year old in America, she wouldn't be around much. I was going to be spending a lot of time alone with the stepmonster.

I eyed the empty desk. I had my laptop and my iPod. My cell completed the package. The whole portable thing was convenient, but it really made it too easy for people to shove their kids back and forth. My dad had let me just spend occasional weekends with him instead of demanding every other week. I was glad. I didn't know how those kids made do with a week at one house and a week at the next. Didn't they get confused when they woke up?

I glanced in Caroline's room as I went back down the hall. Maybe I should bring my TV from home, and then I'd never have to leave my room.

Diane stopped at the end of the hall and said, "You're father won't be home until this evening. I was headed to the pool. You want to join me?"

So, here I was, at the neighborhood pool with my stepmother. It was pretty cool on weekdays in the summer, when just moms and little kids and maybe a couple of teens splashed in the water. Weekends were not so great. On Saturdays, all the beer-guzzling, single businessmen hovered around the pool, stretched out in the lounge chairs. And they didn't concentrate on reading a nice paperback like the women did. No, they sat there and watched. Their eyes tracked everyone as they moved around the pool.

I didn't like all those old guys looking at me. It creeped me out.

A bead of sweat trickled down my chest. Sun-worshiping in August was not for the faint of heart. I had my chair all the way flat in an effort to disappear so I wasn't getting any breeze. At least I didn't have to watch the guys checking me out.

Unfortunately, I couldn't avoid seeing Diane. She was sitting next to me, and she was constantly moving and talking. I tried to keep my eyes closed. She wasn't fat. Actually, she probably weighed exactly what she was supposed to for her height. But she didn't work out. She was soft. And jiggly. She was like forty-something, and she really didn't need to be wearing a bikini. I guess things just started to kind of sag at her age. Whatever the reason, it just wasn't pretty. If she asked me to rub lotion on her back, I'd have to kill myself.

Diane's arm fat wiggled as she reached down to get a spray bottle. "It's so hot today." She misted herself and offered the bottle to me.

"No, thanks. I'm going to get in in a minute." If only someone else would get in. But the other women didn't seem interested. A blonde was drinking beer from a can hidden in a koozie, and the older brunette seemed intent on her book. If one of the men got in, no way was I going to.

The sun burned into my skin, and I was pretty sure I could have toasted a grilled cheese sandwich on my leg. No way was I going to mist myself. That was for wimps and divas.

As soon as I got up, dozens of pairs of eyes would be examining me in my bathing suit. Never mind that I'd covered as much as possible with a simple black one-piece.

The women would be picking my body apart, trying to find something to criticize. And the men, some of them would be looking at me with this creepy intensity that really freaked me out. I didn't want old guys admiring my figure. It was not a compliment. I mean if it's against the law for you to date me, then don't look.

Ignoring the stares, or at least trying to, I rose, waited for the black dots to clear from my vision, and crossed the hot concrete. One. Two. Three. Four. Five. And then I dove in. The quickest way to get covered up and less splash than just jumping.

The cool water was a relief. Too bad I had to come back up eventually to breathe.

When I surfaced and shook the water from my eyes, I discovered that Caroline had arrived and I no longer needed to worry about the unwanted attention. With Caroline around, there was never any left over for me.

Her hot pink bikini emphasized her breasts which actually were not any bigger than mine. Caroline was completely comfortable walking around nearly naked. She didn't crawl into a chair and hide. Instead, she dragged a chair from across the pool over to her mother, scooted it between mine and Diane's, and took her time getting set up. She didn't have the little tummy pouch that I had, but otherwise I knew academically that her body wasn't that much better than mine. But she wasn't afraid of hers. She was two inches shorter and two sizes smaller than me.

I pulled myself up with the ladder and left a trail of water behind me as I crossed the hot concrete.

"Hey, Ally," Caroline said. "I hear you're moving in."

"Yeah," I said.

Caroline settled into her chair, which she kept in almost a sitting position. She started lathering sunscreen on her arms. "So your mom's really moving to Seattle?"

I straddled the seat and sat down. After wiping my face with the corner of my towel, I said, "Apparently." I wouldn't have minded discussing it with her, but I didn't really want to talk about my mom in front of Diane. It seemed disloyal, and if she made any kind of comment, I was afraid I'd lose my temper.

Did I forget to mention that my dad divorced my mom because he was having an affair with Diane? It really isn't easy to like a home-wrecking ho-bag. Mom and Dad both say they would have split up anyway, but still. Got morals? Anyway, I wasn't about to say anything about my mother that would make her look bad. And I really wouldn't tell anything that might make her look, well, pitiful.

"I'll bet it would be cool to live in Seattle," Caroline was saying. "Live bands all the time, coffee houses everywhere, and hot guys."

"Hot guys?" I hadn't seen that on the Seattle website.

Caroline slathered sunscreen on her toned arms. "My friend went out there last year to ski. You should see the guy she hooked up with. Yummy."

"There are plenty of hot guys here in Charlotte, Caroline," Diane said as she reached down for her ever-present bottle of green tea.

"More in Atlanta though," Caroline said.

It wasn't like she didn't always have a boyfriend. She and Diane had lived in Atlanta until two years ago, but Caroline hadn't seemed to have any trouble adapting. At least she didn't go to the same school as me. Being the ugly stepsister every other weekend was way better than twenty-four seven.

"You've never had any trouble with boys, Caroline," her mother chided.

Diane prided herself on her daughter's popularity. That was one of the many things that irked me about her.

"Well, I broke up with Caleb," Caroline said to me. "Did I tell you?"

"No." I'd never even met him. "When?"

She shrugged. "Last week."

She'd have a new boyfriend before school started. I'd bet my bank account on it. And I was saving for a car, so that wasn't chump change. I'd been putting money away since I was eight, and I'd probably have enough for a car by the time I was thirty.

Caroline rubbed some sunscreen into her tan calves. "It's cool, though. He was obsessed with gaming. He didn't even answer his phone when I called sometimes."

"Jerk," I said because it seemed required.

"Tell me about it," she said, finishing up with the sunscreen and laying back in her chair.

I closed my eyes and tried to enjoy the sunshine. Maybe if I pretended I was alone on a desert island. Yeah. That helped.

Later, I was hanging out with Caroline in her Moroccan-themed room when this horrid thudding sound started. At first, I ignored it, but then it started grating on my nerves.

"What is that?" I asked looking up from my magazine.

Caroline shrugged and turned another page, sending a cloud of fragrance in my direction. "It's just Jonathan playing basketball."

Was he in the house with us?

"Oh," Caroline said, her eyes lighting with mischief. She tossed aside her jeweled pillow. "You haven't met Jonathan yet. Have you?" Caroline didn't wait for an answer. She grabbed my hand and dragged me to the door.

"No," I said, adding quickly, "but that's okay. I'm sure I'll meet him later." I knew who he was, of course. I'd seen him next door a couple of times. He was cute. Way too cute to talk to. Well, I thought, glancing at my vivacious stepsister as she led me across the porch, way too cute for me to talk to.

Caroline could talk to anyone, anytime. Even my dad called her charming. And she was already off the porch calling to Jonathan.

"Hey," she said in her deep Georgia drawl that was much more Southern and sultry than my North Carolina accent.

A wide grin lit up the guy's face as he walked over. He tucked the basketball under his arm. "Hey, Caroline. I thought you were gone."

"Just got back. I heard you out here shooting baskets, and I wanted you to meet my stepsister. Ally will be living here for a few months."

"Hi," I said, feeling like an idiot.

Caroline knew how awkward I was with boys. She was too polite to mention it, but I sensed she was on a mission to help me.

"Are you transferring to our school?" He swiped at his messy brown hair.

"No. I go to St. Mary's." The perfect way to kill a conversation—admit you go to Catholic school.

"Oh," he said. His hottiness just starting to hit me full force as he gave me a crooked smile. "Well I'll be seeing you anyway since I'm watching your dog."

Huh? "You're what?"

He gave Caroline a nervous look. "Uh, yeah. I'm keeping your dog at my house, with my, um, dog, while you're at Diane's."

"My dog," I glared past him at Caroline, "isn't staying with me?"

Caroline raised her arms in the don't-blame-me gesture. "I didn't know. No one told me."

Jonathan was antsy. He started eyeing the basketball goal. We'd clearly made him nervous. "I thought you guys knew. Diane and my mom worked it out."

"No freakin' way!" I yelled, knowing it would ruin the unspoken truce I had with Caroline if I said what I really wanted to say. That witch!

"I'm sure she was going to talk to you about it," Caroline said.

Her words didn't ring true, as if even she didn't believe them.

"When did they decide this?" I asked Jonathan in a not-so-nice tone.

He shrugged. "A couple of days ago."

I turned and ran for the house, determined to confront my stepmother before I calmed down and caved in. I'd never put up a fight over anything Dad and Diane did. It just seemed easier to, well, take it. But this was different. This was Mojo and Mojo was not going to be happy staying at some stranger's house. Who knew how they'd treat him or what they'd feed him. Mojo belonged with me. He slept at the foot of my bed and not on the floor. Or, God forbid, outside!

Caroline whizzed past me before I reached the porch. I'd never been a fast runner. I was too tall to be a sprinter.

By the time I burst into the kitchen, Caroline was saying, "Mom! Why didn't you tell Ally about her dog! And why can't it just stay here!"

"Caro," Diane said, looking for all the world like a cornered rabbit. "You know I'm allergic." She pulled the plastic off the top of the frozen casserole and set it on the pan.

"Mother!"

21

"Ally." Diane cut off her daughter with a sharp glance. "I'm sorry I didn't tell you sooner. But I promise you'll see Momo—"

"Mojo!" I snapped.

"Mojo," she corrected with a slight eye roll, "as much as you want. He'll be much happier in a fenced yard."

"He has to stay over there all the time?" I couldn't believe she was doing this.

"Yes. I'm sure he'll be happier there than tied to the tree in the back yard."

Tied to a tree? My blood boiled in outrage.

"Can't he sleep with me? I'll keep him out of your way. He'll be lonely over there at night."

She shook her head. "I'm sorry, but I'm just too allergic. All that dog hair—"

Hair. I could get rid of hair. "I'll wash my sheets every night and do my own laundry. And vacuum every morning before school."

"No. I'm sorry," she said again, but she didn't look the slightest bit sorry. "Jonathan is a nice kid. I'm sure he'll take good care of, um, it."

"I see him out playing with his dog all of the time," Caroline said, trying to be helpful.

"He has a dog?" Uh-oh. "Mojo has to live with another dog?" Mojo did not have social skills.

"He'll have a friend," Diane said, swiping at her eye and smudging her eyeliner.

"Mojo has never gotten along with other dogs. He just barks at them." Or bites them, but I didn't feel like sharing that tidbit.

"Your father thinks he'll adjust pretty quickly. He had dogs growing up, too."

That's right. I'd forgotten that my father was part of this evil scheme. "I guess I'm lucky you guys are letting me sleep in the house." With that bit of satisfying melodrama, I stomped down the hall to my room and locked the door. I hated Diane, and I hated my dad. But most of all I hated my mother for making me come here in the first place.

CHAPTER THREE

When you start off your day in a paper gown, you don't have the strength left for another crisis. —Ally's Brutal Teen Truths

By the time my dad pulled in from the airport at eight, I'd calmed down enough to eat some surprisingly tasty casserole with Diane and Caroline. Dad had been in Phoenix doing an installation since last Sunday. We'd talked on the phone briefly but hadn't really said much of anything. I ran for the front door when I heard the car in the drive.

Diane had been standing at the easel in the living room, and she easily beat me to the door. Caroline was out with friends. So I stood at the top of the stairs and waited for my shot at my dad.

The door opened and Dad gave Diane a kiss on the lips. Uggh. Then he smiled up at me. "Well, this is a nice welcome," he said. "How are my girls?"

I wouldn't be grinning if I were coming home to Diane. Even my mother was prettier. I thought men were supposed to leave their wives for babes, not slightly less attractive women of the same age.

"Are you all settled in?" he asked, climbing the stairs and giving me a hug.

"Yeah," I said. "Dad, we need to talk."

He nodded. "I know, hon. Let me unpack and eat some dinner. You and I can have a little chat."

Then, he turned to Diane and angled his head toward the painting of the blue tulip. "This is new, isn't it? I like it."

Diane beamed. "I painted that in a day. I'm getting faster."

Oh, God.

My father just smiled.

I hoped her painting supplies weren't sucking up my college fund.

"I think I hear my phone," I said, even though I didn't. I ran down the hall to my room and shut the door. I'd done some research on dogs and allergies this afternoon. With any luck, I'd convince my father to let Mojo in the house. Honestly, what did he see in that woman anyway?

I outlined my argument on my laptop. There wasn't any reason to fool around. I was going to be prepared. Dad would hear me out. He always had been good at listening to both sides before he made a decision. I printed my argument on the cheap color printer I'd dragged from home. I'd used bullets and large print. I was ready for battle.

Dad rapped on my door about an hour later. He didn't try the knob but waited for me to open it. I grabbed the paper.

"Hi, hon," he said, his large form taking up most of the hall. "You ready for our talk. I thought we'd talk in my office. We'll have privacy there."

Uh oh. I'd seen enough television to know this was a power play. Meeting on his turf. Unfortunately, the whole house was his. At least the office didn't have any signs of Diane. I'd probably be more comfortable there than anywhere else in this overdecorated house. "Sure," I said and led the way down the hall. Dad was already six four and really fit. The power play on the meeting place was so not necessary.

I jogged down the stairs and through the family room to the office in the back corner. The door was always kept closed to protect his electronics. I turned the knob and entered.

"Have a seat," Dad said, motioning to one of the black leather chairs. Dad's office was mostly black and white. He liked things crisp and clean.

The place even smelled different from the rest of the house. Dad must not allow the perfumed air freshener in here. I sat and he went around the long clear desk to his chair. A counter ran around three walls of the room and held various computers.

Dad gave me a little smile. "So, how's it going so far?"

"Well," I said, unfolding my notes. "Everything's fine except for Mojo. I—"

Dad held up his hands. "Ally, I'm sorry I didn't talk to you about that right away. That was wrong of me. But the fact is that Diane is very allergic to dogs. We were able to make satisfactory arrangements with the neighbor. I know that you're upset, and," he glanced down at my paper, "you've obviously come prepared for this discussion, but I'm afraid there's no wiggle room on this one."

I just stared, open-mouthed. He wasn't even going to listen to me? When I was five, he'd listened to my argument about why I could probably fly off the back deck with an umbrella. And he wouldn't take the time to listen to this? Maybe I should have worn a power suit instead of shorts and a faded t-shirt.

Stand up for yourself, my brain urged. Do it now!

Before I could determine whether or not my body would have listened, my dad started in on this long story about Diane and her allergies. They'd called the vet, and he thought the situation would be fine for the dog as long as I spent time over there with him. Diane had asthma symptoms and they simply couldn't take a chance.

"But Dad—"

He didn't let me talk. He started spitting out words like health insurance, deductibles, allergy shots, and co-pays. It all boiled down to the bottom line with Dad.

Dad leaned back in his chair. "Now that we've got that cleared up," he said.

As if!

"We can talk about this situation with your mother."

He wanted to talk about Mom? He'd carefully avoided any discussion of my mother since the day he'd asked for a divorce and moved out. "We can?" He'd totally distracted me from Mojo.

Dad cleared his throat. "I'm thrilled to have you stay with us here for a few months. I'm not so thrilled about the idea of Karen taking you to Seattle."

Well that made two of us.

Giving me his serious look, he said, "Ally, I'm not sure what I'll do if your mother decides to make this move permanent."

"What do you mean?"

"I don't want to be that far away from you." He spread his hands on the table. "I know we don't see all that much of each other, but the time we have together is very important to me. I don't want to lose that. I don't want to miss your high school years."

We actually agreed about something. "So you're hoping Mom will decide to come back?"

"It's more than just that, Ally. If I wanted to, I could keep her from taking you out of the state."

Well, that was news to me. Could he actually save me from this catastrophic move? "You can?"

He nodded. "I can, but I haven't decided if I will. You could always choose to stay here with me."

I didn't really want to head down this road. He knew some of the reasons I'd probably say no to living with him. "Would Mom agree?"

"I don't know." His serious expression indicated he'd put a lot of thought into this. "I do know that it wouldn't solve your problem entirely. You'd be thousands of miles away from one of your parents either way. And I don't expect you to make this decision yet. As I said, I haven't even decided what I am going to do." Dad shook his head. "I guess I'm just hoping that this doesn't work out and Karen comes back here."

How much did he know about Mom and her plans? "Did Mom tell you that she had him investigated?"

"Yes. As a matter of fact, I insisted on a copy of the report." He stood up and went over to one of the tall filing cabinets. He opened a drawer and pulled out a file folder. "He looks like an average guy, and I think your mother has enough sense to keep out of trouble."

That surprised me. I didn't think he'd admit to Mom having a brain. "So you think she's safe out there?"

Dad sighed. "I think so. Relationships are hard, though. She may decide to come back to Charlotte."

I hadn't expected my father to have a file on Mom's boyfriend. And I hadn't really thought he'd care if I moved across the country. I didn't see very much of him.

MY LIFE AS THE UGLY STEPSISTER

Dad put the file back in the drawer. "I'm exhausted. How about you put on 'Pirates of the Caribbean' and I grab a beer?"

"Works for me," I said, relieved to have the tension level drop. I wasn't giving up on the Mojo situation, but I knew there would be no point angering him until I had a new strategy. "Let me grab my phone and a coke."

"Ask Diane if she wants to join us," Dad said. "Where's Caroline off to tonight?"

I shrugged. "Out with her friends. I think one of them was having a sleepover." Actually, I think she just wanted out of the house. I didn't blame her.

When your mother decides to ruin your life, she goes all out. When Mom called the Monday morning and told me to shower and put on fresh clothes, I should have known I was in trouble. Even though she is a mom, she usually doesn't remind me to put on clean underwear. I pulled a blue miniskirt and striped top out of the closet and dressed. Maybe she was taking me somewhere really cool.

"Is this okay to wear? Where are we going?" I demanded after I got into the car. "What's going on?"

"It's nothing terrible. I promise." The fact that she wasn't driving and wasn't looking at me should have told me to run. "I made an appointment for you at the doctor, Ally." She kept her eyes on the steering wheel as she spoke. "I've been meaning to for a while, and now that I'm going away I didn't want to put it off."

"Oh no," I said shaking my head and reaching for the door handle. "I'm not going to a therapist." I thought they'd given up on a shrink two years earlier. The doctor had declared me to be functioning and not in need of counseling. Of course, I'd told the guy how everything was fine and I didn't want to talk about anything.

"No, Ally." Mom finally turned my way. "I want you to be comfortable with this process in case you need to go. I think you'll like Dr. Peeden."

Dr. Peeden? Wasn't that her... My jaw dropped in horror.

"Yes, Ally. My gynecologist."

I crossed my legs. "Mom! No! Why? What did I do?"

"Nothing. It won't be bad. You'll like her, and if you need her over the next few years you'll be able to call her."

"You aren't going to be gone for years."

"No, but my mother took me when I was twelve. For my cramps. I want you to go before you develop a fear of it. Some of my friends never go, and that's not healthy."

Now the clean panties thing made sense. "But I'm fine. Advil works for my cramps." Four of them, but still they did work. "I'm not going."

"What if you get a yeast infection while I'm gone?"

Eewww! "I'll use the cream they show on television. I'll stop eating sugar. I won't get a yeast infection."

Mom shrugged. "Go with me now or go with Diane next week. It's your call."

"You're never coming back from Seattle, are you? You just want to do one last thing before you abandon me."

Mom rolled her eyes. "I'm not abandoning you. You know better than to think so."

I did know, in a way. Mom really liked being a mother.

A half hour later, I was shivering in a paper gown with an equally useless paper blanket pulled over me. Why were they blasting air conditioning in a place where they made you strip naked? I was starting to regret making my mother stay in the waiting room. The whole thing was gross and embarrassing and the longer I waited the more I agonized. I didn't even want to look at what was "down there" and no way did I want someone else staring between my legs.

Mom had tried to break the tension by telling me a story about one of her friends whose doctor thought she was flirting because she accidentally covered her... self... in glitter. Something about her kids and not realizing they had used the washcloth for the mess they'd made. "So don't you worry," Mom had said. "These doctors have seen it all."

Well, they hadn't seen me, and I was happy with the status quo. I squeezed my legs together. Very happy.

Finally, the doctor knocked. She introduced herself and shook my hand. I didn't want to think about where her hand had been.

She was younger than my mom, with short blonde hair, a white coat, and a smile that was probably meant to be reassuring. She seemed nice enough. "Are you having any problems at all?"

"No."

She asked when my last period was, and whether I did self-breast exams.

"Um," I said. I'm not a very good liar.

"You should do them every month."

"Okay."

"First, I'll check your breasts. I'll call in my nurse, and then, after that I'll have you put your feet up in the stirrups for the pap smear."

Stirrups?

The nurse came in, and Dr. Peeden had me lay back and raise one arm above my head. She pulled the paper gown aside and began very scientifically rubbing my breast. Then she did the other one. I pretended it wasn't happening. Apparently, she didn't find anything wrong. But I'd seen my breasts. The parts at the other end of the table were the ones I hadn't examined closely. Who knew what horrible secrets they held?

The stirrups were even worse than they sounded. I had to scoot my naked butt down to the edge of the table and put my feet in the metal things so that my legs were spread wide. I felt ridiculous, and the warm lamp she had shining on me did not help. The sun was not supposed to shine down there.

Why stirrups? Was the first gynecologist some kind of sick cowboy? I mean really!

Obviously they kept you spread open for the doctor to access you, but still...

"This is the speculum," the doctor was saying. Apparently she hadn't seen any shocking deformities with her bright light so far. "I'll slide this in to keep you open for the pap test. Then, I'll use a cotton swab to get some cells from your cervix. It won't hurt," she assured me.

I tensed, like any reasonable person.

"You'll have to relax," she prompted. "Just lay back and think about something else. It will make it easier."

Somehow, I managed to relax a little. She slid the thingy in and then did the thing with the swab. I was really picking up the technical lingo.

"You're doing great," she said.

She released the speculum thing and took it to the sink. "Next is the bimanual exam. I'll place two fingers inside your vagina, and then press with my other hand on you abdomen to feel your uterus and ovaries. It won't hurt, either."

"Great," I said. Sounds delightful. Mom had done this every year since she was twelve?

I was starting to feel kind of violated. Even though I knew it was all legitimate. And my mother was right. It was over with faster than a trip to the dentist.

"We're all finished here." Dr. Peeden stripped off her gloves and threw them in the trash. She turned off the light. "Go ahead and get dressed. And I'll see you in a year."

Yeah. Right.

"Don't forget to go over those pamphlets on the HPV vaccine with your mother."

Mom took me for lunch at my favorite restaurant and then bought me two new CD's. It didn't buy her my forgiveness, but I wasn't going to turn down good stuff either.

I'd already been through a lot today, so I tried to convince her to wait on introducing Mojo to Jonathan's dog.

"I don't want to put it off, Ally." Mom said when we pulled up at our house. "We need to know if they hate each other so I can make other arrangements."

I wasted no time ejecting my CD and sticking it in the gem case. "Like forcing Diane to let me keep him in the house?"

Mom grimaced. "No. Like find someone else to watch him."

We'd already had two hours of discussion about Diane and Mojo. Mom couldn't force Dad and Diane to do anything. Of course Mom thought keeping him next door was absolutely reasonable since I'd get to see Mojo as much as I wanted.

Watching two dogs sniff each other's butts didn't sound good to me after being felt up at the gynecologist. Dealing with a cute guy was enough of a challenge when I hadn't just had a woman's hands all over me. When you start off your day in a paper gown, you don't have the strength left for another crisis.

Mojo greeted me excitedly when I entered the house and I rubbed his head. "Hey, baby," I said in my puppy dog voice. "You want to go meet a new friend?"

Mojo seemed to like the idea because he jumped up with his paws on my stomach, but then he had no clue what I was saying. He didn't usually play with other dogs and when I walked him and he sniffed other dogs in the park, well, he tried to eat them. So no pressure. The chances of him getting along with Jonathan's dog were...great.

The way my life was going, I really just wanted to hug my dog, cry, and hide under my bed. I ran to my room, wiggled out of my skirt, and pulled on a pair of shorts. Mojo wagged his tail as he followed me back to the door.

My dog loves to ride in the car so Mom keeps an old blanket over the back seat. Sometimes Mom takes him along when she's running errands. The drive-thru at our bank will even give him a dog biscuit. And sometimes, the guy at Wendy's gives him a free burger. My friend says they chop up the overcooked burgers and put them in the chili, but every now and then one goes to Mojo.

I hooked his leash to his collar, and he practically bounced off the walls. He jumped right into Mom's Camry, and I shut the back door. I knew better than to ride over there in the back with him. He liked to run from side to side to see out both windows. I climbed in the front, and we headed over to my dad's.

Dad and Diane had bought a house as far away from ours as possible in Charlotte. I wondered if they'd opened a map and done it on purpose. Probably. It would be just like Dad to do something like that. And I wouldn't put anything past Diane.

At home, we didn't have a fence for Mojo. I just walked him every day, and he sometimes stayed on a line outside. I knew it would be good for him to get to run. It was just the being away from him part that worried me. Well, that and the other dog. It didn't matter which one came out on top. If they fought, it would be bad for me. And Mojo.

Mojo stuck his black and brown head between the seats to see out the front, and I rubbed behind his ears. Years of experience had taught me that this would keep him from jumping into my lap, or worse, my mother's.

I struggled to rid my mind of this morning's activities as we drove across town. Jonathan wasn't that hot. I could probably manage. Maybe.

Mojo sighed as if to disagree.

Yeah, I didn't believe me either.

CHAPTER FOUR

No way will you escape your teens without being humiliated. A lot. —Ally's Brutal Teen Truths

We pulled up in front of Dad's house, and I grabbed the leash as Mojo bounded out.

"We're only fifteen minutes late. Jonathan and his mother are expecting you. I'll be back in an hour," Mom said from behind the steering wheel.

"What?" I turned back, gripping the leash. "You're leaving?"

Mom's expression turned guilty. "Well, you don't need me to help with the dogs. And I really don't want to drink tea with Diane for an hour."

Oh. Good point. I nodded. "Come back in an hour." I wouldn't want to drink tea with her either. And she hadn't stolen my husband.

With the smile of an escapee fresh from Alcatraz, Mom said, "Thanks, hon. And good luck."

"I'll need it," I grumbled. I led Mojo to Jonathan's front door, dodging a tiny bicycle on the sidewalk. A lawn mower buzzed down the street, and the scent of freshly cut grass tickled my nose.

Jonathan answered before I could knock, and I took a step back. "Hey, Ally. So this is Mojo." His smile was kind of nice. His orange Charlotte Bobcats t-shirt revealed hints of muscles in his arms.

He leaned down and talked to Mojo before petting him, instantly making friends with my dog. But was he really a dog-lover, or was this just a show?

I finally managed a "Hi." Then, I remembered I was on a mission and got my wits together. "I never asked what you were getting for doing this," I said.

He gave me a guilty wince. "Braves tickets. Diane's ex-husband had season tickets and she got them in the divorce. We're going to Atlanta at the end of September and we're catching a bunch of games."

Baseball. Those tickets were probably worth hundreds of dollars.

I was just starting to get irritated with him when he said, "I would have done it for nothing, but my dad needed something to justify all the fuss."

"What fuss?"

He motioned to Mojo. "He'll probably bark at night at first. Until he gets settled."

"He doesn't bark." Mojo had gotten bored and sat down.

"Even if he's outside with another dog and someone walks by with their dog?"

I winced. "Okay, maybe then he would bark."

Jonathan smiled. "It'll be cool. Buddy could use a friend."

"You named your dog Buddy?"

A little color rose in his cheeks. "Uh, my little brother named him."

"Oh."

"Let me bring Buddy out front. We can see how they do before we try putting them in the fence together."

I dragged Mojo around the front yard and he peed on every bush we passed. "You're on empty," I told him. "Get over it."

Jonathan's dog led him through the gate on a mud-splattered leash. Buddy was a little smaller than Mojo. He was a tan mutt, and he got right to business sniffing Mojo's butt.

At first, Mojo was too busy with his nose in Buddy's rear end to get upset. Then, he growled and started to attack. "No, Mojo," I snapped, holding tight to the leash.

Jonathan dragged Buddy a few feet away and we tried again. "Give them a minute."

But Jonathan looked up and met my eyes and suddenly I couldn't think. He had the most beautiful liquid brown eyes. Like the amber glass beads on my mother's favorite bracelet.

My family had green eyes. I'd always thought of brown as dull, but his were beautiful.

Unfortunately, he was still talking and I had no idea what I'd missed.

"Huh?" I said, like a total dork.

His lips curved into a smile. "I said let's put them together in the fence and let them play."

This time Mojo tried to hump Buddy. My face flamed.

I'd never been so embarrassed in my life. "Sorry," I mumbled to Jonathan after we pulled the dogs apart. "It's not a sexual thing, you know. It's about dominance." Oh my God. Had I really just said that? To a guy?

Jonathan laughed. "It's normal. Don't worry about it. I've had Buddy for six years. I've seen a lot of, um, humping."

We stood awkwardly watching the dogs romp around the back yard. Jonathan was standing, but he wasn't still. He seemed kind of edgy, like he was as uncomfortable as I was. He kept fidgeting and moving. Putting his hands in his short pockets. Taking them back out. He swiped at the lock of chestnut hair that had fallen across his forehead.

"They seem to be doing okay, now." Mojo and Buddy were running at full speed around the back yard.

"Yeah, uh." Jonathan bounced in place. "Do you want to sit down on the porch?"

"Sure. I guess." A couple of chairs and a long metal swing, practically a couch, with big cushions formed a sitting area on the back patio.

Jonathan pointed to the swing. "That's Buddy's bed. I wouldn't recommend sitting there."

I stopped. "Why? Would he growl at me?"

"No. It's just really not clean."

With a last glance at the sofa, I sat in one of the chairs. The seat was warm, and the sun beat down on me as I tried to make conversation. "You go to Plum with Caroline?"

"Yeah."

Silence. An uncomfortable silence followed. The sun-lightened hair on his calves between his knee-length athletic shorts and running shoes drew my attention.

"So you go to Catholic school?" he asked.

I nodded. "My grandmother insisted. Dad was raised Catholic, but they didn't have a school where he grew up. My grandmother prays the rosary every day. She's beyond devout. She's practically a saint. She probably won't even have to wait until she dies to get into heaven. They'll probably just beam her up or something." Why was I babbling?

"Do the nuns rap you on the knuckles with a ruler? I always wondered."

"No. We only have one token nun. The rest are just normal teachers. And we have Mass every morning and religion class every day. It's really not that different. Plus, they used to paddle kids at public school."

He shuddered. "Thank God they don't do that anymore."

"My dad took a few beatings."

The sun brought out the different shades of brown in his hair. "Do you have cliques just like public school?"

"Probably worse. We've been with the same kids forever and there aren't that many of us. Everybody wears the same uniform but you can tell who's rich by their jewelry and their purse. There are a lot of doctor's kids."

He raised a brow. "Catholic guys carry purses?"

I rolled my eyes. "Just the girls. And before you ask, mine is a Target special. I don't own a Dooney and Bourke. I don't have two hundred and fifty dollars for that crap."

"Two hundred and fifty bucks!" His jaw dropped. "For one of those ugly purses. You've got to be kidding me."

I shook my head.

"Do you know how many games I could buy with that?"

I shrugged. "A lot?"

"Five. Five brand new games for my Xbox 360." He looked at me with a hopeful expression. "Are you a gamer?"

"Not really. I like playing, but not enough to spend all my money on it."

The sliding glass door opened behind us and a woman came out with a little boy at her heels.

"You must be Ally," Jonathan's mother said with a big smile. "According to Diane, we'll be seeing a lot of you around here."

"Yes," I said, feeling stupid. "Nice to meet you." She didn't look much like Jonathan, but the little boy did.

The little boy ran straight at Jonathan's knees like a runaway train. Jonathan scooped him up, turned him upside down, and made him giggle. His Spongebob Squarepants t-shirt fell over his angelic face revealing an adorable tanned tummy.

"This is Ben. He's four," Jonathan's mom said. "And you should call me Marianne."

I nodded. "Thanks for keeping Mojo here."

"No problem. Bill, my husband took the bribe, but Jonathan and I love dogs. Ben too." She had chin length reddish hair and wore a striped blouse, capris, and sandals.

Jonathan had righted Ben and set him on the ground. "Mommy," Ben said, running over to her. "Can I play with Buddy?"

"Not right now, Ben. Remember how we talked about it. Buddy has to get to know his new friend first."

Ben pouted.

His mother turned to me. "I just wanted to say hi. I'd better get the rugrat back inside." She moved back toward the door.

"Thank you," I said, not at all sure what to say.

"Go with Mom, Ben," Jonathan said when his brother didn't follow.

Ben gave a dramatic sigh and went in with his mother.

I looked at Jonathan who'd sat back down. "So, Ben named Buddy, huh?"

Jonathan froze.

"Two years before he was even born?"

"Uh, yeah." Jonathan's knee bobbed up and down. "Okay, so I named him. But in my defense I was only seven."

I cracked up. He was so busted. Buddy! "Not real original of you."

"Hey," he said gracing me with a grin. "You named your dog Mojo. Is that for voodoo? Or Austin Powers?"

Crap. "Actually," I lowered my voice, "it's for MoJo Jojo."

"What?" He scooted his chair closer.

"Mojo Jojo."

"I can't even hear you. Just say it." He moved another foot in my direction.

"Mojo Jojo. You know from the Power Puff girls."

Jonathan busted out laughing.

"It's not that funny. Look at his face. He sort of looks like a brown and black monkey. Just like the villain on the cartoon."

"That's just," he laughed so hard he could barely speak, "sad."

I put my hands on my hips. "I was only eight." Okay, so I was ten, but he doesn't have to know that. "It's not like I'm a devoted fan or anything." Anymore. "It's just the name of my dog." Mojo dashed over to lap up some water from the giant bowl and then ran off again.

Jonathan's eyes met mine, and I could see the curiosity mixed with his amusement. I was starting to feel less insulted and more, um, like I was just realizing how really cute Jonathan was.

"Okay," I said. "We were both lame. How about we never mention this again. To anyone?"

"Deal," he said and held out his hand.

I was used to shaking hands with my mom and dad's friends, but not with guys my age. Okay, don't be wimpy. Don't think about how cute he is.

I reached out and took his hand. Both of us had dog slime on our hands anyway, it wasn't like...

Oh. I stopped breathing. It totally was like holding hands. Like my skin against his. Only it wasn't going to last long enough.

My eyes met his, and I got lost for a minute.

He recovered first, released my hand, and twisted to get a look at the dogs.

I wouldn't have noticed if the dogs had morphed into dragons and flown away.

My mouth was parched from the sunshine or the contact, or both. I jumped up. "I should probably get Mojo and go."

He stood reminding me that he was several inches taller than I was, his height a perfect complement to mine.

"Right." He gestured to where the two pets were playing. "I think they'll be okay."

"I'll bring him next week," I said, backing away. "Thanks for helping. If my aunt kept him in Knoxville, I'd never get to see him."

"No problem."

It turned out that there actually was a problem because Mojo wouldn't stop playing to let me hook him on the leash. "He doesn't really mind," I admitted.

"He doesn't even come when you call him?" His tone of voice brought the word incredulous to mind.

"Well, yeah. Usually." He came if he was in the mood to come in, which was never.

"Buddy comes when I call him. He's not really trained, but he can do that."

"Prove it," I said. "Maybe if he comes to you, then Mojo will get close enough for me to catch him."

"Good idea," he said. "Buddy. Here Buddy."

His dog-calling voice was kind of cute. The melodic sing-song quality made him seem a lot more vulnerable.

Especially when Buddy took one look at Jonathan and decided not to come.

His cheeks turned red and he wouldn't look at me. "Buddy," he called in a firmer tone. "Get. Over. Here."

I cracked up. I couldn't help it.

Jonathan gave me a sheepish grin. "He, uh, usually comes."

"He's probably just distracted by Mojo. Maybe I should call Buddy and you should call Mojo."

He shrugged. "Couldn't hurt."

"Buddy," I said walking towards the sliding glass door. "Buddy." I felt stupid using my dog voice in front of Jonathan. Before I could glance at Jonathan, Buddy came running right up to me.

"Traitor," Jonathan muttered.

I leaned down to pet Buddy, and Mojo ran up to get my attention back. I grabbed his collar, and hooked on the leash.

Buddy decided to pay attention to Jonathan since Mojo couldn't run off and play.

With a grin, I said, "Piece of cake."

He rolled his eyes. "I think maybe two dogs are more than twice the trouble."

JULI ALEXANDER

I started toward the gate with my dog, and Jonathan held Buddy's collar while we went out. "Thanks again," I said. I really didn't want to get a crush on this guy. Crushes never turned out well for me.

I scanned the street in front of Dad's house, but Mom's car wasn't there yet. I guessed I'd have to go in and talk to Diane.

The sound of an engine coming from the other direction caught my attention and I turned. Mom pulled up to the curb in front of Jonathan's house. I strode over and opened the back door. Mojo bounded in, and I climbed in the front.

"You left your cell phone in the car," Mom said. "I've been waiting forever."

"Really? How long's it been?"

"I've been here for twenty-one minutes," Mom said.

So why was she just pulling up. Unless... "Were you hiding down the street?"

"Yes," she said unapologetically. "I stopped about six houses down and watched for you." To the eye, she was a perfectly coordinated and confident woman. Inside, apparently, not so much.

"I know you didn't want to see Diane, but you could have come and got me."

"I didn't want to interrupt." She eyed me over the top of her sunglasses. "How'd it go? Do you think they'll get along?"

"Yeah," I said, reaching back to pet Mojo. "They did good."

"It probably helps that they've both been neutered. They should do that to men."

"Mom—" I started.

"I know," she said. "What would Dr. Phil say?"

But she was grinning as she pulled away from the curb. "How about spending the day with me? I'll take you back to your dad's tonight."

"Sounds great." I grabbed some moist towlettes from the glove compartment to wipe off the dog slime. I rarely got to hang out with Mom on a weekday, and I wanted to spend some time with Mojo. He probably thought I'd left him for some stupid guy. Like my mother was leaving me. Oops. Being bitter. I could almost see myself blowing Mojo off to spend time with Jonathan, and that scared me. I'd never teased a guy before and

40

had him tease back. I was pretty sure I'd been flirting, something I would have sworn I couldn't manage to do.

CHAPTER FIVE

Boys will always notice your hot stepsister first.
—Ally's Brutal Teen Truths

Caroline was hanging out downstairs in the family room when Mom dropped me off. "Hey," she said, from her cross-legged perch on the couch. "I'm glad you're here. I'm bored to tears."

"Where's your mom?"

"In bed with a migraine."

"Oh, sorry." I couldn't quite work up any compassion for Diane.

"Come sit," Caroline said, patting the chocolate brown leather sofa.

I sank onto the sofa, the leather cool from the air conditioning. "How was your trip to your Dad's," I asked. "I forgot to ask yesterday."

"It was good." Her spaghetti-strapped tank showed off her arms. "Zack got into trouble though." She lowered her voice. "He took my dad's car out joyriding."

The younger stepbrother. "He's what, fifteen?"

She nodded. "He hasn't even got his permit yet. Dad was furious. Apparently a cop pulled him over on the Perimeter."

"I thought your stepbrothers got along with your dad."

"They do. I don't know what's gotten into Zack. But now the whole house is under lockdown. And Nick, who's seventeen and does have a license, is furious about it." She tucked a chocolate curl behind her ear.

"He's being punished too."

"Technically, no. But Dad's being all vigilant now and asking where he's going all the time. Nick used to pretty much do what he wanted."

"Wow. A lot happened while you were there."

She glanced at the stairs and then said, "I was hoping to stay there for a while."

"You were? Don't you like it here."

She shrugged. "I like it fine, but I miss my dad. I haven't seen much of him except in the summers."

Her life wasn't perfect? Well, other than her ho-bag mother. "So why'd you come back?"

"Dad was so stressed out, he probably wouldn't have noticed me anyway." She got this serious look. "I know you live in the same city as your dad, but you don't see him too much. Don't you miss him?"

Here was a tricky question. I had to avoid the whole hostile feelings over the affair discussion. I thought for a minute. "Not much has really changed for me, I guess. Dad traveled all the time, and he wasn't there much. I saw him some on weekends, and we did stuff. Now I see him almost as often." I'd only recently figured out that my father was probably spending so much time away from home or at least busy in his office in the house in order to avoid my mother. It wasn't a pretty thought.

Caroline nodded slowly. "I see what you mean. My dad was always around. He owns his own business, so he took off a lot during the week when things were going on. He never missed anything at school. We used to just hang out a lot."

I couldn't imagine hanging out with my dad much. Even before the divorce, our relationship had been kind of distant. Like he didn't know what to make of a daughter. He was kind of obsessive about the computer stuff and he'd get lost in it for hours. I guess he had his head in the clouds a lot. And I was always busy doing my thing too or hanging with my mom. Mom and I liked the same movies. To see a movie with Dad, one of us had to compromise. It was just easier with Mom.

This was the most Caroline and I had ever talked about real stuff. Things had always been awkward between us because of our parents. She clearly projected a warning that I shouldn't talk about her mother, and I shot one right back that said,

43

"Don't tempt me." Now, I felt for Caroline. "Can't you go down for some extra weekends? He'd probably go for that, right?"

She looked thoughtful. "Yes, but it's hard with everything going on. I don't want to miss all the fun stuff at school. I'm going out for junior varsity cheerleading, so I might have games a lot on Friday nights."

"That's cool," I said. "I'm sure you'll make it."

"I've been practicing. My back flip isn't good enough, but my back-walkover is solid."

Caroline had taken gymnastics for years. She was two inches shorter than me, but everyone told me I was too tall. I took it in pre-K and never again. Of course, I was a chubby kid. Maybe they just didn't want to put me through the humiliation of wearing a leotard.

"What are your plans for your freshman year? You start at the high school right? Will it be any different?"

I nodded. "Two other schools feed in, so there will finally be some kids I haven't known since kindergarten. I'm thinking about going out for soccer. I'm not that good, but the junior varsity team is pretty desperate. Two of my friends play."

"That sounds fun. I never tried soccer. Mom always put me in gymnastics and cheerleading."

"You like them though, right?"

"Yeah." Her face lit up. "Guess what else I like. I met this guy today at the pool. His name's Liam, and he's a junior at my school. Have you met him?"

I shook my head. I'd never met anyone named Liam. "I doubt it. I don't know many people at Plum High."

"He is so hot," she said with a dreamy expression. "I'm going to try to find out more about him. Leslie thinks her brother knows him. Of course, he's a junior and I'm just a freshman."

If any freshman could snag a junior, it would be my stepsister. "So how'd you meet him?"

She shrugged. "He just came over and we started talking. Then, he challenged me to a diving competition." With a grin, she said, "Of course, I won."

She could dive really well. All that gymnastics paid off on the springboard.

"I promised him a rematch tomorrow. Will you come?"
What else could I say? I had no plans at all. "Sure. I'd like to meet him." I'd rather run a marathon than meet a seventeen-year-old guy while wearing my bathing suit. But whatever.

We ordered three movies in a row on pay-per-view. My dad would probably kill Caroline and me. Between us we drank six Diet Cokes and ate two bags of popcorn. And a couple of mini Snickers bars. Then, I drifted off somewhere around two, halfway through the third movie.

When Caroline woke me, we hurried upstairs to slip on our bathing suits. Diane had apparently recovered from her headache. She was spraying some kind of toxic stuff on one of her paintings to preserve it or to make it even uglier. I wasn't sure.

I coughed as I followed Caroline down the stairs. My stepmother couldn't handle some dog hair, but she didn't mind breathing those fumes. Yeah, her asthma was really bad. I was so sure.

By the time we trooped to the pool, there were six of us. Four of Caroline's friends had come to view the hot guy. Having them around didn't make Caroline nervous. I doubted anything did. She must have been born with a talk-to-guys gene.

After we claimed some chairs, Caroline hit the pool. She executed a double flip and dove into the water. I'd have been afraid the teeny bikini top would come off. She wasn't. And it wasn't that she secretly wanted to lose her top. She didn't need to pull stunts like that to get guys to drool over her.

Liam couldn't take his eyes off her. Neither could his two friends, or for that matter, any of the men at the pool. And it didn't freak her out. She just kept diving, talking, flirting, and having fun.

I sat in a chair surrounded by Caroline's friends, Chelsea, Kelsey, Haley, and Barbara. I know, Barbara's mother clearly hadn't gotten the memo. Kelsey and Haley were big flirts, but Barbara and Chelsea were more down to earth. They were all pretty and popular and going out for cheerleading. Chelsea and Haley were blonde. Barbara had dark brown hair and wore an orange bikini that looked great against her dark skin.

"So, Ally," Kelsey said. "Are there any hot guys at your school we should meet?"

I thought for a second. "Probably. And there will be a bunch of new guys this year because St. Frances and St. Luke feed into St. Mary's too."

"Oh, not freshman," Kelsey said with exaggerated horror. "If I'm dipping into private school, he has to be at least a sophomore."

"I'll keep my eyes peeled," I said, imagining prying out my eyeballs and throwing them at Kelsey.

Barbara gave me a commiserating smile. I decided right then that she was my favorite.

Haley turned her attention away from the guys for a minute. "Kelsey? Didn't you say you were going after Caleb?"

"I'm keeping my options open," she said.

"It's never good to date Caroline's exes," Haley agreed. "I've done it twice, and they just go on and on about her."

I laughed at that. Kelsey deserved Caleb if that was the case.

If I did meet a guy who was decent, I'd introduce him to Barbara. It wasn't likely, since I'd never actually established any kind of friendship with a boy. I'd spent more time with Jonathan than anybody else. How sad was I?

"Ooh!" Haley squealed. "There's Jonathan and he has his little brother with him."

My heart froze. I was not ready for socializing in a bathing suit. Not with him! I actually kind of liked him.

The girls next to me waved and across the pool, Jonathan waved back. He had Ben by the hand and was carrying towels and a beach bag.

"He's such a sweet guy," Barbara said.

"Yeah," Kelsey agreed. "But he's a freshman."

My heart must have started beating again at some point because I didn't pass out, but I gripped the sides of the chair and prayed that he'd stay far away.

He did. Luckily Ben insisted on getting straight into the pool. Jonathan set his burdens by the fence, kicked off his shoes, pulled off his t-shirt, yum, and helped Ben shed his shoes and shirt. Then they jumped into the shallow end which was thankfully far enough away that I could pretend he didn't really see me in my bathing suit.

Caroline and Liam were splashing around in the water, and she squealed as he picked her up and tossed her. Everyone turned that way. Caroline splashed at him, then climbed from the pool for another dive.

My eyes darted to Jonathan who had one hand on Ben, but his eyes were glued to Caroline. His mouth was open as if in awe. He kept staring until Ben splashed him in the face.

Here was the familiar pain of the crush. Jonathan was hot for my stepsister just like everyone else. My heart felt like it had been run through the cheese grater.

I pulled on my t-shirt and gathered my things. "I'm heading out," I said to Caroline's friends. "See you guys later."

"Bye," they said.

I slipped my shorts on and jammed my feet in my slides. Without another glance toward the pool, I made my way out the gate.

CHAPTER SIX

Seeing your stepmother naked is even worse than seeing your mother naked. –Ally's Brutal Teen Truths

I walked four blocks to my dad's house with the sun beating down on me. By the time I got there, I had worked up a sweat and really could have used a dip in the pool.

The air conditioning hit me in the face when I opened the door. Much better.

I took the stairs two at a time and turned the corner to head for my room. Then I saw something so horrible, so undeniably grotesque that I knew I'd never have a good night's sleep again.

Diane stood in the hall butt naked. She was pulling a towel from the hall closet, and I had the full side view of the droopy breasts, tummy sliding down an inch or two, and saggy buttocks.

Bile rose in my throat, and I made some sort of whimpering noise.

"Oh. Hi, Ally," Diane said, turning to me as if this weren't the worst experience ever. She held the towel, folded in a neat square, but didn't bother to open it. "Back so soon."

I looked at the floor, my feet, my hands, anything to clear my head of the images. Diane stood her ground. Almost as if she were proud of herself.

Surely she didn't think she looked good? Surely she wasn't trying to hit on me.

"I, uh, yeah."

She held the towel at her waist and I was grateful for the six square inches it concealed. "I was just thinking of heading that way."

"I, uh, yeah." Not hitting on me. Just proud of her ugly body.

She had me trapped. Should I run screaming for the front door? She was blocking my room. Should I just bolt past her?

She was walking closer to me. "I was going to look down in the laundry room for my suit. I think it's hanging down on the rack."

"Okay," I said averting my eyes and holding my breath as she walked right past me to go down the stairs.

She pranced right down as if there weren't windows around the door. As if I weren't standing right there. As if she weren't butt naked.

I shuddered. I thought seeing my mother naked had been bad, but this was much worse. Mom would have covered herself. Anyone would have covered themselves! I had to live here for four months with a wicked stepmonster who was some kind of wrinkled, saggy streaker? I ran for my room. Was she one of those nudists? Did she belong to a club where they all got together and sat around naked? Screw this. I was going to Seattle with my mother.

"Ally," my mother said a few minutes later. "I can't talk right now. I'm training my replacement and I have all kinds of loose ends to tie up."

"Mom, this is life or death." Seeing something that shocking and ugly could kill someone. If I were older, I'd probably have had a heart attack. Or a stroke. As it was, I had post-traumatic stress disorder. "Help me."

"I can't believe she'd really just parade around like that, Ally. Surely you're exaggerating."

I lay on my back on the twin bed with my pillow over my eyes. "I'm not!"

"I'll call you as soon as I get off, honey. Right at five. We'll talk about it then, but I don't think it's a good idea for you to come with me to Seattle. You can put up with Diane for a while to stay with your friends and your school. You're just not thinking clearly."

I agreed and hung up. How could anyone think clearly after that nightmare? I couldn't even close my eyes. I kept seeing it. Over and over. This was how I was spending my last few days of summer?

I powered up my laptop and checked my email. Then I slipped out of my bathing suit and put on shorts and a t-shirt. When I heard the front door slam, I figured the coast was clear of naked old people. I went to the kitchen, grabbed a drink and a sandwich, and headed downstairs for the big TV.

Mom called at five. She agreed to let me come home the next day. "Do you want me to talk to Diane?"

"And say what?"

Mom sighed. "I guess that you're uncomfortable."

"What good would that do?"

"I'm not sure."

"Forget it," I said. "I'll live." My heart was broken. My eyes were burning, and my stomach kept threatening to toss back the sandwich.

I called Madison and MC, short for Mary Catherine. Both of them expressed the appropriate degree of horror. They agreed to come hang out with me at my mother's tomorrow.

When Caroline asked me later why I was leaving early, I told her that my mother missed me. "She didn't want to waste any more of our time together."

"Oh," Caroline said. "That makes sense."

"I'll be back next Friday." We'd both start school by then. "We can catch up on all the back to school stuff."

The last week of summer went pretty well. I got to hang out with my friends. We went to Madison's pool a lot. There was no one around but us, so I wasn't uncomfortable.

I relaxed on a giant hot pink float next to Madison. "This is way better than being at my dad's." I inhaled the scent of coconut sunscreen and soaked up the rays.

"Oh, yeah. You never told us about that guy who's watching your dog. Is he cute?" MC asked from the side of the pool.

"He's okay." I didn't want to get into it. "He's like everybody else in the world. He has it bad for Caroline."

"That sucks," Madison said, running her fingers through the water. "I thought you guys might end up liking each other."

"At least you'll get some practice talking to boys," MC chimed in. She was treading water beside us. MC swam like a fish.

"You know what else she needs practice with," Madison said.

"Hello? I'm right here."

"You need practice standing up to your parents," MC said.

"Oh, don't worry. I'm totally turning over a new leaf. I'm tired of getting kicked around. I'm tired of taking it. When I get back to the house of shriveled saggy naked people, heads are going to roll." I had actually worked up something of a tirade.

"Good for you, Ally," Madison said.

Besides hanging with my friends, I slept in my bed, and got to hang out with my mom. I went shopping and spent a fortune on new clothes. When I heard the total at Anthropologie, I was afraid Mom would pass out. But she just whipped out a credit card.

"You'll need extra," Mom had said. "To keep up with Caroline on the weekends. She has more clothes than you do since she doesn't have the uniform."

Mom was right. I usually had three pairs of jeans I liked and a few tops. Caroline had a much more impressive wardrobe. I'd spent a good part of the last two years green with envy over her outfits.

So now I flipped through the clothes in my closet wishing I could wear something cool for the first day of school. Instead, it would be the green and Navy plaid skirt and white blouse. At St. Mary's, the girls wore oxford-style shirts like the boys. Only dweebs wore the girl version of the white blouse. Girls and boys were allowed to wear navy blue pants and red, white, or green polo shirts. Madison had it on good authority that it was considered uncool to wear pants. We didn't want to start high school on the wrong foot. MC's sisters had been conflicted on the issue. We went with Gina's opinion. She said pants were fine if you never wanted a date because nobody looked good in the boy-cut uniform pants.

Of course, the new, pleated skirts fresh from the factory looked a little dweebish themselves. We had to wear knee socks year round. I'd gotten in the habit of wearing shorts under my skirt in kindergarten. I wondered if I should keep that up. If someone noticed, would I be ostracized? No way was I flashing my panties. That was so Lindsay Lohan wannabe.

The week should have been great, but instead I felt like a cloud was hanging over me the whole time. This could be the last week of my life as I knew it. And at the very least, I was headed back to the middle-aged nudist colony. Eeew. The ugliness.

Sure, I'd be seeing a lot of Jonathan, but I'd have to watch him leering at my step-sister. Life so was not fair.

The over-starched skirt was already itching me when Mom let me out of the car on the first day of school.

"Have a good day," she called.

"Thanks," I mumbled, looking around for my friends in the sea of green plaid.

"Ally," MC called from behind me. "We're over here!"

Thank God. I couldn't begin to imagine facing high school without my best friends. If I moved to Seattle, that's exactly what I'd be doing. "Hey guys," I said, joining them near the flagpole in front of the dingy, old brick building.

"Listen, Ally," MC said, motioning for me to lean in closer. "I've been thinking about your stepmother. Do you think she's a lesbian?"

"No," I answered honestly. "I think she's just a freak."

"Even if she were a lesbian," Madison chimed in, "she wouldn't hit on Ally and risk her husband finding out."

"Okay, then, this plan only works if she's not a lesbian," MC said. "If you're going to have to see her naked anyway, why not do something to make her look better."

Huh? "Like what?"

"Like buy her a toning video, or some classes or something."

"Eeww. I don't care how toned she is! It's major ick either way."

MC shrugged. "Just trying to help."

"Oh, oh!" Madison grabbed my arm. "I know. Give her the video anyway. To insult her. Now that you've seen her naked, it would be totally bitchy to do that. But what could she say?"

Now that was a plan I could embrace. To insult her. Call her old and flabby by giving her a workout video. What could she do to me? And even for a mega bitch like her, it would have to hurt. I grinned. "I would love that!"

"Really?" Madison acted shocked.

"You don't think I can be obnoxious."

MC snorted. "We know you can be! But not to an adult. Even your stepmonster."

"We have to get it right after school, before you back out." Madison clapped her hands. "This is going to be great!"

"Come on," MC said. "We'll be late."

I followed them through the door of the school. We were supposed to go in the gym for homeroom assignments. We didn't have our class schedules yet, so who knew if we'd be together at all. "Are your skirts making you itch?"

They answered a firm no, and I started to wonder if mine was infested with some kind of bug. Mom had washed it, hadn't she? I'd be a big hit if I spent the first day of my freshmen year scratching myself. Hives would be even better. Or swarms of scary insects jumping off my skirt. Okay. I took a deep breath. No way was I giving Diane that video. I could barely cope with life now. A guilty conscience would do me in. Darn Catholic school!

I knew a few kids in my homeroom, but they had us sit in alphabetical order so it didn't really matter. With my schedule in hand, I headed out to the hall. I popped my lock on my assigned locker outside homeroom. If only I had made plans to meet up with MC and Madison to compare schedules. We'd signed up for most of the same classes. Maybe we'd gotten lucky.

Geometry was my first class, which was good I guess because I'd be a little alert to do the math. I located the classroom and walked in with my fingers crossed. Well, mentally at least. I said hi to a couple of the brainy guys I knew from eighth grade. I grabbed three desks near the back, securing one with my purse and one with my backpack. I plunked my butt down in the third. Then, I waited. Several girls and guys came in who must've come from St. Luke.

My three least favorite girls from St. Catherine with the latest Coach bags, matching of course. And finally, MC and Madison. I held in my squeal.

They rushed back to me.

"This year is going to be awesome!" MC said with her typical optimism.

"New guys," Madison whispered with a nod of her head.

She was right. Two cute guys had just walked in. Actually, they practically strutted with confidence. They must have been from St. Luke's. I thought Jonathan was probably cuter though.

MC grinned. "Me like."

I knew MC could get any guy she wanted. She just hadn't wanted anyone at our old school. The youngest of four girls, MC was just a tiny bit spoiled and had years of training in the art of flirting. Her family wasn't rich, but they adored MC. She had this sense of entitlement that I envied.

For now we had a mission. Find out who these guys were.

"After nine years of the same people, we finally have fresh..." Madison trailed off.

"Meat?" MC asked.

"Blood?" I offered.

"Boys," Madison said with a big smile.

I relaxed in the old-fashioned wooden desk. Helping them stalk these guys would keep them from noticing my real crush. So far, they'd accepted my story that I didn't care about Jonathan.

Overall the day went pretty well. I met a girl named Katelyn in my French class. She seemed pretty nice. I knew someone to sit with in all my other classes. I had four with Madison and three with MC. By the time school ended, they'd forgotten the insulting present for Diane.

Soccer tryouts were next week, and I hadn't decided what to do yet.

Tonight I made my semi-permanent move to Dad's. Mom was taking a flight out first thing in the morning. My nerves about the first day of school had kept my mind off my domestic issues. But as I walked to Mom's car in the car pool lane, the doubts and fears crept back in.

How was I going to survive four months in the den of the naked stepmonster?

Three boxes and two large suitcases were crammed in the backseat of Mom's car when she picked me up. "You loaded all my stuff?"

"I hope you don't mind. I'll stay at your father's for a while and help you unpack," she said pulling away from the curb.

"You don't have to."

She put her hand on my knee. "Yes, I do. You'll know if I forgot anything. Plus, my flight isn't until midnight."

"Hey," I said as I realized my dog wasn't there. "Where's Mojo?"

"He's fine. I went ahead and dropped him off. I couldn't fit everything in the car with him along."

"He's at Dad's?"

"No. He's at Jonathan's. I made arrangements with his mother, and she put water and food out back for him. They're keeping Buddy in until Jonathan gets home."

I thought of Mojo all alone in a strange back yard and felt like I might throw up.

"He'll be fine." Mom patted my leg again. "Really. You'll be there soon. He's going to adjust to the situation. We all will." She sounded kind of wistful as she said it. "I made sure they had all my contact info and Mojo's vet records. I also put a copy in the box for you."

How very paralegal of her.

When we pulled up at my dad's, Diane opened the door and came out. "Make yourselves at home," she called. "I'm going to run over to the school and get Caroline."

I was glad to see she had clothes on, but her top had a plunging neckline that belonged in a nightclub and not a carpool lane. My mom had on a trendy black track suit with pink piping. Mom looked casual but sophisticated and very much like a mother. Her breasts wouldn't tumble out while she helped me unpack.

"Oh, I'm sorry," Mom said. "Did we hold you up?"

"Oh no," she waved away Mom's concern. "I'll be back in about thirty minutes."

I watched her climb in her car and back out of the driveway. "I think she was running away from you, Mom."

"Good," Mom said. "Uh, I mean, don't be silly." She gave a little fake laugh.

"Pretend you never said that?" I asked.

"Please." She scooped up my laptop and a big suitcase and headed into the house.

Mojo must have heard us, because I heard whining and scratching on the nearby fence.

"Go ahead and check on him," Mom called over her shoulder. "I'll unload the car."

"I'm coming Mo," I said. I set down my backpack and purse and stepped into Jonathan's yard to the gate.

I couldn't see him behind the tall, cedar fence, but I was already smiling at his greeting. I opened the gate and slipped in. Mojo jumped up putting his front paws on my waist. He wasn't supposed to do that, but I didn't mind.

"Hey baby," I said, leaning down to hug him. He kept wiggling around excitedly. "Do you like it here?"

In response, he ran to the gate and jumped up like he was ready to go.

Oops. "No, sweetie. You're staying here."

I guess I was totally wrapped up in comforting Mojo because I didn't notice Jonathan until he was right beside me.

Jonathan had his hands in the pockets of his shorts. "He settling in?" he asked.

"Hard to say," I answered, suddenly aware that I still had my uniform on. Oh, right. It didn't matter anyway. He had a thing for Caroline. I could relax. He would never look at me that way.

Mom chose that moment to open the fence and peek in. "Are you coming?"

"Yeah, Mom. Just a minute." I motioned to Jonathan. "Have you met Jonathan yet?"

"No. Nice to meet you," my mother said, her big smile showing off her newly whitened teeth. "I'll take another load up, but we need to get you settled. Then you can see to Mojo."

"Okay."

"I'll throw a ball with him and Buddy while you do that," Jonathan said. "Maybe it'll distract him."

I smiled at him. "Thanks. I guess I can't do everything at once."

"C'mon, Mojo," he called. "Let's play." He started walking across the yard and Mojo followed before he noticed that I was slipping out the gate.

I heard him run after me with a bark of dismay. "Be right back, boy."

When I got upstairs, Mom said, "You didn't tell me he was cute!"

Darn her for noticing. "He is?" I tried to sound vague and detached. I don't think I quite got there.

"Maybe this won't be so bad after all, Ally. You'll have Caroline and then there's a boy handy to drool over—"

"Mom! I don't drool over boys."

She shrugged as she folded one of my shirts. "Whatever you want to call it these days, girls will always have a thing for cute boys."

"I don't have a thing," I stammered. "He seems nice enough, but he's just watching my dog. Besides, he's slobbering all over Caroline."

Mom slid a pile of clothes into one of the dresser drawers. "He isn't watching Caroline's dog."

"What? Was that some kind of marriage contract in the medieval village you grew up in? Watch the dog, marry the girl?"

Mom couldn't help laughing. "Me thinks thou dost protest too much."

I put my hands on my hips. "I'm not discussing this matter any further."

With a grin, she straightened the clothes on the hangers. "I want you to be happy."

"I know." Then because she seemed to be getting melancholy again, I said, "He is a little bit cute."

"I knew it!"

Mom had just pulled away when Diane drove up with Caroline. I wondered if maybe she had hidden down the street like Mom. Nah. Diane had no shame. Plus, Caroline would totally bust her.

Caroline ran through the door and gave me a quick hug. "I made the cheer squad!"

"That's great!" I pushed the words out, trying for some enthusiasm. I had a lifelong problem with sounding excited. I don't know why, but I freeze up when I know I'm supposed to gush. "I knew you could do it."

Caroline seemed to think I did well enough. She dashed down the hall to her room. "I have four more phone calls to make. Then we'll catch up."

Her door closed, and Diane came in. "I thought she'd bounce right out of the car."

"She's pretty happy."

Diane's thin fish lips curved into a smile. Her eyes lit with pride. "She sure is."

I guess Caroline never mentioned the part about wanting to stay in Atlanta. As I walked back to my room, I realized I had several weapons I could use to make Diane feel like crap. I wouldn't use them, but it was nice to have options.

"I'm going to run next door and check on Mojo," I told Diane after changing into shorts.

"Tell Jonathan hello for me," she said in this teasing voice.

For a minute, I wondered if maybe she was trying to fix me up with Jonathan. Then I realized that she was actually just trying to make me think she was cool enough to kick my dog out as part of a matchmaking scheme. Pretty crafty, but I wasn't buying it.

I opened the gate expecting to see Jonathan and the two dogs. Since I'd be over here a lot, I needed to get used to talking to him. I could talk to one average guy, right?

But the one guy had turned into three. Jonathan had two of his buds sitting with him on the porch. Mojo was soaking up the attention from the tall blond. I wasn't ready to face three teenage guys. I wasn't Caroline.

"Hey, Ally," Jonathan called. He'd probably noticed me backing toward the gate. "C'mon over and meet Dave and Colin."

I managed to get out a "Hey," and the two guys answered with heys of their own.

Mojo left his new best friend and ran up to me. I leaned down to hug him.

"Your dog's cool," Dave said.

"Thanks." Maybe this wouldn't be so impossible after all. The guys weren't the least bit uncomfortable having me there. They seemed very cocky.

"So, dude," Colin said. "She's here now, so can we hit the PS3?"

Jonathan turned to me and back to his friends.

"I'll take over here," I said. "I'll make sure these guys," I gestured to the dogs, "are okay."

"Thanks," Jonathan said with relief.

Was he relieved because he didn't have to stall his friends any more or because he could ditch me?

They went inside and I picked up the discarded tennis ball. I threw it, and Buddy got there first. Instead of bringing it back to me, he ran in circles while Mojo chased him barking at the top of his lungs. They were having a blast, but my head was starting to pound. My dog was really causing a commotion.

I heard the sliding glass door behind me and thought Jonathan had returned. Instead, I found Ben slipping out the door.

"What are they doing?" he asked in his baby-like voice as he tugged at his Spiderman t-shirt. "They're driving me crazy."

I laughed at his pained expression. "I think they're playing keep away."

Buddy finally noticed Ben and ran over to greet him. Mojo took advantage of his distraction by stealing the ball. Buddy ran after him barking like Mojo had done.

"Ouch," Ben said.

At least this time it was his dog making the noise.

"Dad was right," the little boy said. "Two dogs are a lot louder than one."

Ouch.

CHAPTER SEVEN

Boys get distracted and confused by breasts. Even old wrinkly ones.
—Ally's Brutal Teen Truths

When Diane had come over to fetch me for dinner, Jonathan and his friends had been out shooting hoops. I was glad they made enough noise to drown out some from the backyard.

She opened the gate a crack and called my name. I petted Mojo and told him I'd be back after dinner. He ran off after Buddy, so I figured he was okay.

When I got to the driveway, I saw that Diane was flirting with, I mean, talking to the guys. Jonathan was being all polite to her. Dave and Colin were staring at her cleavage, blushing, looking away, and then staring again.

Eewww! And I'd been worried that they'd think I was a loser. Hello! Big losers. Totally leering at Diane's old lady boobs. Gross!

"Hi, Ally. I was just telling Jonathan here how much we appreciate his help with Momo."

"Mojo," I muttered.

Jonathan glanced at me then back at Diane, and I could see that he was working really hard to keep his eyes trained on her face. The way she was dressed, you almost had to look at her breasts. Even I had found myself ogling them, and I had zero interest. Mine were much nicer. The wrinkly skin above them really turned me off. Puke.

"See you guys later," I said and hurried past Diane to the house. Talk about a creepy situation.

Diane made grilled chicken. It looked way too pink to me, so I just cut it up and moved it around to look like I ate it. No way was I getting salmonella for this woman.

"Caroline," Diane said, after chewing her piece of chicken for a long time. "My friend Susan has a kitten she's trying to give away."

"You hate cats," Caroline said.

"I was just thinking that it's too bad you don't have a pet."

Caroline put down her fork and said in this firm voice, "But you're allergic, remember?"

"Well, yes," Diane said, sounding strange. "Cats don't bother me as much as dogs. There's something different about the dander. But I was thinking maybe one of your friends could take it. The kitten."

Huh? Had Diane really just tried to talk Caroline into a cat? I pretended I hadn't heard the conversation. I was really glad I hadn't made an effort to eat the chicken.

After dinner, I spent two hours doing my homework and getting ready for school the next day. Mom had put most of my stuff away, so I had to hunt down my hairbrush. I found it in the desk drawer. As if that made any sense.

I checked my email and replied to MC and Madison. I was beginning to understand why guys were so freaked out about their penis size. At least, Cosmo said they were. I'd gotten so much spam about it that I was starting to feel inadequate. And I didn't even have a penis. No wonder guys were so messed up. I checked out the new pictures on MC's Facebook and left Madison a message that I loved her new background. I had to dodge a few more weirdos. The coolest part about the whole site is the free music.

After shutting down my laptop, I went out to check on Mojo. He wasn't as happy as he'd been earlier. Buddy wasn't either. He was whining at the back door. They probably usually let him in the house by then.

At ten-thirty I showered, changed into clean shorts and a t-shirt, my usual PJ's, and slipped beneath the yellow coverlet. I closed my eyes as my head sank into my soft pillow. I tried not to think of my poor lonely dog. I didn't buy the allergy excuse. The flowery fragrance of Diane's laundry detergent and ever present air freshener made my nose itch. How could she breathe it in all the time if she really had allergy problems? The cat thing was the last straw. No way was she suggesting Caroline's friends take the kitten. I didn't know anybody who was allergic to dogs but not cats. As my nasal passages threatened to seal shut, I couldn't help picturing Mojo's sad face as he realized I was leaving him tonight.

I'd never had to deal with this much crap at once. School starting should have been a big enough stressor. Staying here, missing my dog, worrying about my mom, avoiding my stepmother...It was a bit much for a high school freshman.

I gave up at eleven-thirty when Buddy and Mojo started barking incessantly. I grabbed my cell phone just in case somebody called. My friends usually avoided calling me in the middle of the night because I get really grumpy when somebody interrupts my sleep. I opened the door to my room and listened for a moment. I didn't hear a thing. I'd already said goodnight anyway so Diane wouldn't come looking for me. Surely my luck wasn't so bad that I'd run into her on my way out the door.

Since the front door squeaks, I crept out the back. I walked around to the front yard and opened the gate to Jonathan's yard. The loud sort of chirping, buzzing sound from the woods behind the house covered the sound of the wood scraping as I opened the gate. Vicious barking came toward me at an alarming speed until Buddy and Mojo realized it was me.

"Hey, boys," I said, taking care to pet both of them. I talked puppy talk to them for a few minutes and then went and sat in one of the chairs on the back porch. Mojo sat right against my right leg and Buddy my left. The night was warm and calm, and I wasn't freaked out by the darkness with two dogs to protect me. Not that they would. They'd both probably give a murderer big sloppy kisses as he chased me around the yard. Still, it was comforting in a strange way. I felt peaceful. I never felt that way in my room at my dad's.

The darkness grew blacker, and the buzz of chirping from the woods grew louder. Whatever it was, turned out to be comforting. Me and the dogs just chilled. I didn't hear anything from inside the house. The family room was dark inside the sliding glass door. I wondered which room was Jonathan's. Was he in there asleep? Or was he tossing and turning like I had been?

Eventually, I stopped petting the dogs and they lay down at my feet and dozed. My mind drifted to school and the new kids, and English class where I didn't know anybody to sit with. I knew a few kids but none I liked. I wished I could just snuggle up with Mojo in my room at home. My butt was falling asleep in the hard chair, and I would have loved to stretch out. I squirmed a little, thinking how tired I was going to be in the morning. Hopefully dark circles under the eyes were considered cool.

Yeah, I didn't think so either.

Finally I realized no blood was circulating in my rear end. I didn't want to end up with a butt cheek amputation, so I pulled myself up and stood. The dogs immediately came to attention.

"Sorry, Mojo," I said with a yawn. "I've got to go to bed. You stay here with Buddy."

I petted each of them one last time and walked toward the gate. They ran along with me hoping to play. Until I got close enough to the gate that they figured it out.

Mojo started whining and Buddy barked at me. Mojo joined in the barking.

"No. Shhhh."

They didn't shush.

I winced and started backing away from the fence. "Shut up you guys! You'll wake everybody up." I doubted Jonathan's parents wanted me lurking in their yard after midnight.

Crap! I gave up and ran back to the porch. Mojo and Buddy gave a few last barks, of joy if I wasn't mistaken, and then calmed down.

If I was stuck here, I was going for the swing where I could stretch out. Buddy would just have to share.

I sat on the swing and swung my legs up onto the cushions. I leaned back, not too sure what I'd be putting my head in, but I was too tired to care. Buddy jumped up instantly and rested his head on my chest. Mojo must have realized we were in Buddy's territory because he settled for climbing up next to my feet.

I hadn't even realized I'd been getting a little cold until the heat from the dogs warmed me up. A blanket might have been more effective, and more sanitary, but I was resigned to spending the night on the porch.

Buddy raised his head an instant before the sliding glass door opened. I jumped but didn't bother getting up. Running away would look even stranger than lounging with the dogs.

Jonathan slipped out the door. "Hey, I wondered if they were barking at you."

In the dim light, I could see that his hair was tousled from his pillow. My heart thumped in my chest. Buddy stayed put. I guessed he was comfortable.

"Sorry," I said in a half-whisper. "They started barking when I tried to leave. So I thought this would be better."

He eyed me and my two bedfellows for a minute. "You guys look pretty comfy there."

I was hoping he couldn't see me blush in the darkness. "I, um, tried the chair at first, but no way could I spend the whole night in that."

"You do know what they say about lying down with the dogs."

One of my dad's favorite sayings. "Yeah, I know. I'll get up with fleas." Yuck. "Mojo's been treated. Plus, that's really just an expression, right?"

Jonathan smiled. "Buddy usually sleeps in my bed. So I think you're pretty safe."

"Did we wake your parents up?"

He shook his head. "I doubt it. I'm just really tuned in to Buddy. I expected him to have some problems, but I didn't want Mojo to have to be alone. Dad drew the line at two dogs in the house."

Poor Buddy. He'd been booted out because of Mojo.

"It's okay, though," Jonathan hurried to say. "Buddy is having a blast with another dog around."

Hopefully, he meant it and wasn't just trying to make me feel better. I didn't know whether to stay or go. "Mojo will probably be okay now, if I go..." I didn't sound the least bit convinced.

"Do you want me to stay out here so you can go home?" he asked somehow reading my thoughts. "I don't mind sleeping here if it would make you feel better."

"No. I don't really mind staying. I hate to make you do it." I was afraid he'd argue, so I said, "Besides, it isn't really home over there anyway."

"At least let me get you a blanket and a pillow. I'll set my alarm for early so you can leave before my parents wake up."

"You don't—"

"It's the least I can do," he said and slipped back into the house.

He didn't seem to think I was a total freak for sleeping on his patio.

He came back loaded down with blankets and pillows.

"Thanks, Jonathan. It's really not that cold out here." It was still August after all. The nights were cooler but not cold.

He handed me a blanket and pillow and then set another pair down on the ground. "Be right back," he said.

I tucked the pillow under my head relieving the tension on my neck. Much better. Then I covered myself with the blanket as much as I could without burying the dogs. After just the vinyl cushions on the metal frame, the bedding felt decadent.

Jonathan came around the side of the house carrying a cot.

"The swing is fine, Jonathan," I said when he reached me. "But thanks."

"The cot's for me," he said, setting it up a few feet away and putting the pillow and blanket on it. "I'm not letting you have all the fun."

I couldn't help grinning. "You're sleeping out here with me?"

"That's the plan."

He really was nice. Or else he just didn't want Buddy hanging out with me all night. "Are you jealous?" As soon as the words were out of my mouth, I realized he probably thought I meant jealous of the dogs because they were in bed with me. "I, um, mean because Buddy's hanging out with me."

"No." I thought I heard a trace of laughter in his voice. "You're welcome to him. He snores."

Buddy gave a loud sigh.

I giggled. "He says you're lying." Relaxing a little, I sank into the cushions.

"You'll see," Jonathan said as he lay down on the cot.

It wasn't until he was lying down that it hit me. I was practically sleeping with a guy. Sure, it was innocent, but it was also strangely intimate. Being out in the darkness, late at night, stretched out with our pillow and blankets.

It was kind of magical.

"So was today your first day of school?" His voice sounded different somehow when he wasn't standing up.

"Yeah. It was okay." Were we really going to have a conversation? "What about you? You started yesterday."

"It seems okay so far."

"You didn't get knifed already? You know that's what they tell us at parochial school, that the public schools are crawling with knives and guns. Plus, with you being a guy, and a freshman, there's probably a whole gang of delinquent seniors out to kill you." He didn't look like a freshman to me.

His deep laughter filled the air and teased my ears. "As far as I know, nobody wants me dead. Yet."

"I'm sure Sister Teresa would say it's just a matter of time."

"She could be right."

Sister Teresa was never right. "So, are you going out for basketball?"

He rolled over onto his side and tucked his arm under his head. He seemed even closer to me. "I don't know. Probably not. I'd rather play church league. The competition's pretty fierce for junior varsity at Plum. I might wait until next year."

My church was my school, so it was weird to think of them as two separate things. "What church do you go to?"

"Well," he said quietly. "We go to a Methodist church sometimes. But I play over at the Presbyterian church with a bunch of my friends. They do a lot of things with teens...lock-ins and stuff."

"That's cool. I get tired of the people at my church. You know, because I see them all the time."

"You can come over to Second Pres. Everybody's welcome. I don't know if Caroline's been there or not. She probably has though. Lots of kids from Plum High and Jefferson Middle go. You could ask her about it."

Caroline's been everywhere. I didn't welcome the reminder. I didn't have the guts to ask if he had a crush on her; plus I knew he'd never tell me the truth. I wouldn't want to embarrass him when he was being so nice.

"It must be pretty cool having a stepsister your age. Not like having a bratty little brother."

How on earth did I answer that one? When I didn't say anything, he asked, "You get along with Caroline, don't you?"

"Oh, yeah," I answered. "She's nice to me. It's just weird. My dad only married her mom two years ago. And with us being the same age...I don't know. It's just, weird."

He was quiet for a minute. "I hadn't really thought about that. Do you like Diane?"

I groaned. "I'd really rather not answer that question."

"I think you just did."

"Don't mention anything to Caroline please. She probably suspects how I feel, but it would be rude to actually say it."

"No problem. I see you way more than her anyway. The only time I see Caroline is when she's dashing from the door to the car."

With a smile, I said, "She does have an active social life."

"But then don't we all," he said, and I totally got that he was mocking himself and not just me.

"My social calendar takes up all my RAM memory," I teased.

"I have to keep track of mine on the walls of my room."

I could picture his walls covered with appointments and parties. "Like your parents would let you do that."

"What are they going to say to me? You should see what Ben's done with crayon in the living room."

Having a little brother would be fun. "He's a cute kid."

"He's okay."

I started to offer a trade—Ben for Caroline. Then I realized he might take me up on it, and that would tick me off.

I'd grown accustomed to the chirping noise, but it stopped and suddenly started again. "What is that buzzing noise anyway?"

"Frogs," Jonathan answered. "The woods are full of them."

"They must be to make that much noise. How'd you know that?"

"Two years in the Boy Scouts."

I'd done a year in the Girl Scouts, but it wasn't my thing. "You'd think they'd stop being sexist by now, and just have Scouts."

"No way," Jonathan said in a teasing voice. "Girls have cooties. Besides, girls can join the Boy Scouts in high school. There's a branch called the Explorers."

Coed Boy Scouts? I'd never heard of it. "So they like go camping and hiking and stuff."

"Yes. You could join. My friend Colin goes on hikes all the time."

Uh, yeah. "I'm not actually that into camping and hiking."

"Then why were you complaining?"

"I just think girls should have the choice. Do you know what the Girl Scouts is like? Cookies, crafts, and singing songs in rounds just didn't do it for me. That doesn't mean I want to sleep with the snakes and bugs."

"You're sleeping outside right now," Jonathan pointed out.

"Yeah, but I'm steps away from air conditioning and bathrooms, and cold beverages."

"That's true."

"Plus, you can't take your dogs camping with the Scouts." I scratched behind Buddy's ears.

"True," he said looking over at the dogs. "They look pretty cozy cuddled up with you." And I thought I heard him murmur, "Lucky dogs."

"What?"

"Nothing."

A wide grin nearly split my face. He had said it.

"Ally?"

"Yeah?"

"Good night."

I pulled the covers up to my chin and tried to stop smiling. "Good night, Jonathan."

Loud barking penetrated my sleepy fog and I opened my eyes to see that it was daylight. I squinted at the brightness. I must have left my blinds open. My roof open? I was outside?

"Buddy doesn't like it when people walk or jog by our house," a deep voice said from next to me.

What the—. I heard some kind of squeaking sound coming from myself. Then I remembered. Jonathan, the dogs, slept on the porch. I turned my head to see Jonathan sitting up on the cot facing me.

"I didn't mean to scare you," he said swiping at his eyes.

"Uh, no." I struggled to sit up, swung my legs to the ground sending the swing creaking and swaying, and perched on the edge for a moment.

The barking got really vicious.

"Somebody must be walking their dog," Jonathan said. "Buddy really hates that."

"What time is it?" I reached for my cell phone even as I asked.

Five forty seven. "I better run. Your parents aren't up yet?" I did not want to see what they thought of our sleeping arrangements.

"No. I don't think so."

I pushed the woven blanket aside and jumped up. The cover was a peculiar shade of orange. When my breasts started jiggling from the sudden movement, it hit me that I wasn't wearing a bra. I was braless and standing right next to a boy. I crossed my arms over my chest, but Jonathan hadn't noticed. He was already grabbing the cot and folding it up.

"Go on home, and I'll stash this stuff."

"Thanks, Jonathan." I took off at a run for the gate. The dogs chased me, abandoning their campaign against the joggers. Leaning down, I gave each of them a pseudo-hug. "I'll be back after school," I said to Mojo. Then using my leg to hold them back, I went out the gate.

The last thing we needed was two dogs running loose through the neighborhood. Especially when neither would come when we called.

CHAPTER EIGHT

When you have to buy tampons, there will always be a hot, young guy at the register. -Ally's Brutal Teen Truths

Twenty seconds later I slipped in through the back door and hit the stairs at a run. I was at the hall bathroom when the door to my dad's room started to open. I darted into the bathroom and started the shower to avoid discovery. But as long as I was there I may as well wash all the dog hair off.

As I shampooed my hair with Caroline's expensive shampoo, I tried to wrap my mind around my life. This had to be the weirdest morning. I'd slept outside with a boy. So far I hadn't gotten busted, and it was fun. Hanging out with Jonathan, and our dogs of course, was pretty cool.

The thing that I didn't quite get was why Jonathan had come outside with me. He didn't have to. Did it mean something? At the very least, it meant that he was a good guy right? And if it meant more? What did it mean? I'd never been friends with a guy. And a guy had never liked me. Well one had, but I hadn't liked him back. For one thing, he was even more of a nerd than me. And for another, it made me way nervous that he liked me.

But anyway, Jonathan was not a nerd. He was a total hottie. I finished in the shower and grabbed my robe from the hook on the bathroom door. I'd had Mom buy me one after the Naked Incident with Diane. Maybe she'd learn from my example of modesty. Oh, crap and there was that grotesque image again.

Ewww.

I grabbed my cell out of the drawer where I'd put it to minimize the impact of all the steam. Then I headed to my room. Diane passed me in the hall.

"Good grief, Ally. I thought Caroline was bad. Even she doesn't take her cell phone in the shower with her."

I just smiled like she was being funny. I'd had next to no sleep, but I didn't feel tired. I felt excited and special. I was so developing a big crush on Jonathan. He was extra cute in the morning with his husky voice and tousled hair.

I closed the door and sat down on the bed. Ooh. Soft. Too bad I couldn't move it out to the yard next door.

Or move Mojo in here. And that was what was really bothering me. Last night was way cool. Was I going to have to tone down my outrage at Diane? After all, her ridiculous allergies were the reason I'd seen Jonathan. Last night. This morning. Almost every time come to think of it.

A tap on my door barely registered before a bleary-eyed Caroline came in. "G'morning."

"Hi."

"Oh good," she said as she took in my robe and wet hair. "You already showered. I wanted to be sure we both had enough time in the bathroom. Did you bring your blow-dryer, or do you need mine?"

I hadn't bothered with things I'd known she'd already have. "No. I need yours. Sorry. I usually don't wash my hair in the morning so I wasn't thinking."

Caroline sighed. "I guess we're going to have to get up this early every day."

"I'm not really a morning person," I admitted.

"Me neither," she said before giving in to a huge yawn. "I'm jumping in the shower. I'll leave the door unlocked in case you need something."

"Thanks." The downstairs bath in the laundry room wasn't conducive to getting ready.

I dressed in my uniform and got the blow dryer from the bathroom. I sat at the desk and dried my hair. When Caroline got out of the shower, I did the whole wash your face brush your teeth thing. Caroline appeared in the bathroom door in a cute t-shirt and jeans. She pulled out three different brushes and got to work.

Caroline either had some natural talent for make-up and hair, or she'd snuck into a L'Oreal training program one summer. Maybe the whole modeling thing she'd done had hooked her up with some training. She'd said the whole print ad thing was boring and time-consuming, so she'd quit. Whatever the reason for her skills, she put me to shame. My half of the counter held one hairbrush (I mean really shouldn't one be enough?), a toothbrush, face wash, blush, eyeliner (which I rarely used), and lip gloss. Applying eye shadow was far beyond my capabilities. Sure, it looked easy, but it wasn't.

My hair looked great though. Her snazzy shampoo really did the trick. I watched Caroline as she finished her hair and started on her makeup. She didn't just put on base, blush, eye shadow, eyeliner, and three different lipsticks. She did some kind of shading and blending thing. Had she learned this from her mother? Because it really wasn't working out that well for Diane. She looked hideous even with all the makeup.

"You can use anything you want," Caroline said, not for the first time since I'd known her. She selected some eye shadow and lipstick. "These would look good on you."

"I'm not all that good at putting on eye shadow."

"Oh, well I know all kinds of tricks. I can show you, maybe tonight?"

"Okay. I guess I'll grab some cereal."

Caroline laughed. "Oh, no you won't. Mom's on a new kick. She's cooking."

We walked into the kitchen together to see Diane wearing...an apron?

"Hi girls," she said wielding her spatula. "I made soy sausage patties and egg-beaters. And wheat toast." She smiled like she'd done something amazing. "Sit down."

We each took a seat at the kitchen table and she served us some shriveled up egg-looking things and fake sausage. The sausage wasn't bad. The eggs...I wouldn't have fed them to Mojo.

I wouldn't have fed them to Diane.

We all piled into Diane's Land Rover. She chatted about some guy coming to buy her kiln and pottery wheel. I resisted the urge to ask how much of my college fund she'd wasted on making the two crappy, crooked pots that cluttered the shelf over the stove. We dropped off Caroline first. I searched for a glimpse of Jonathan but of course he wasn't among the sea of students outside Plum High.

My buds were waiting for me again in front of St. Mary's. They gave me a Buns of Steel DVD from Madison's mother's collection. I slipped it into my backpack and pretended to go along with the plan.

MC's sister had some info on one of the hotties from yesterday. She was friends with his sister. For some reason, I didn't want to tell them about last night yet. A girl has to have some secrets.

At lunch, the soccer coach, Coach Borkman, came up to our table in the cafeteria and asked me to try out. I hadn't played since fourth grade. I wasn't sure I could even do it. I hadn't exactly been the star player back then.

MC and Madison acted all engrossed with their lunches, but I knew they were to blame. Madison hadn't played in years either, but she had decided to try. Of course, Madison was way more athletic than I was.

Coach Borkman, who didn't look like a coach at school in her skirt and floral blouse, pulled out the chair next to me and sat down. "Here's the thing, Ally. I need a team of at least fifteen on JV. I've only got twelve girls signed up."

"I haven't played in years," I told her. "I'm not really that good."

Coach Borkman sighed. "I'm going to be brutally honest with you. Right now, I just need warm bodies. If all you did was just stand on the field and never touch the ball, it would still help us out."

Warm bodies. I could probably do that.

"Having said all that," she said, raising a brow, "if you decide to come out for the team, I expect you to make it top priority and give two hundred percent at every game and practice."

"Okay," I said. "I'll give it a shot." Why not? I needed to exercise anyway. It wasn't like it was wasting any of my time.

MC and Madison cheered.

"Thank you, Ally," the coach said. "This is the first year of our JV program. It's a building year for us. I don't want to lose the opportunity."

It wasn't until she walked off and I took a bite of my peanut butter and honey sandwich that I realized what her quest for warm bodies really meant. She was looking for bench warmers.

Fine by me. I couldn't make a fool of myself on the bench.

Diane was waiting in the carpool lane when school got out. She didn't know about the exercise video I had in with my books, but I still felt uncomfortable. She informed me that she had two art classes and an art show that night. Dad would be home around six. Caroline was heading out with the cheerleaders after practice.

Basically, I was on my own. I would have loved to hang with MC and Madison, but I couldn't spend the night and abandon my dog.

On the phone later, MC didn't understand.

"I don't get it. Your dog is fine. Besides he doesn't know the difference if you're at your Dad's or at my house."

I certainly wasn't going to explain it to her. Oh, gee. I'm actually sleeping in the back yard now with the dogs and the boy. No. Uh uh. "It's hard to explain," I said.

"Fine. Why don't I just come over there and spend the night? Your dad won't care, right?"

This was even harder to explain away. Because Dad and Diane would totally let me have MC spend the night. But then MC would know what I was doing, and I didn't want her to know yet. And with a guest over, Diane might check on me more. And Caroline might feel like she had to hang out with us. It was a chance I couldn't take. "Maybe next weekend," I said. "I don't want to rock the boat yet."

"I thought you were all about rocking the boat," MC said. "Remember? The whole tired of taking it speech?"

She didn't understand, but she'd forgive me.

I was nervous about seeing Jonathan again. Were we friends now, or would it be all awkward like usual?

Dad ordered Chinese for dinner, and we ate together. Apparently, Diane had sold him on the green tea. He was drinking it when she wasn't even around. The Dad I knew had been a solid Coke man. He told me about his week in Miami. He asked about Madison and MC whose names he still couldn't remember with any regularity.

"Have you got plans for tonight?" Dad asked, relaxing at the table in khaki shorts and a knit shirt. He liked to be comfortable at home.

"Not really. You?"

"I'm three episodes behind on Mad Men. It's me, the remote, and the Tivo tonight. You're welcome to join me, but you'd probably rather visit with Caroline and her friend."

Great. I knew Dad got sick of staying in hotel rooms. "Sounds like fun." It didn't, but I had my own never-miss shows too. I'm not a big Mad Men fan. Now if only I had something to do tonight.

Caroline had Haley with her when she got home. They were talking a mile a minute and giggling. Haley's parents had to be rich. She was too full of herself. I knew she wasn't a natural blonde, but I'd never been able to catch her with any roots. She obviously had regular salon appointments.

"Hey, Ally," Caroline said. "We're gonna hang in my room. Wanna come with?"

Uh. "In a little while. I've got a couple of things to do."

I checked on Mojo again, but I could only spend so much time in the neighbor's yard. Jonathan wasn't around, but his parents were. His mother kept coming out like she felt an obligation to talk to me. I finally gave up and went back to Dad's.

I had mixed feelings about the chatter from Caroline's room. I'd like to hang out, but I didn't much like Haley. Plus, I didn't want to be the annoying unwanted sidekick. Caroline didn't dislike me, but I didn't want to push it. On the other hand, I didn't want her to think I was blowing her off. It was a fine line, and I doubted I'd manage. I'd probably have to go in there for a while. Then I could visit Mojo and claim to be wiped.

I had complete confidence that I'd manage to tick Caroline off in no time.

Then disaster struck. A painful sensation in my abdomen that could only be a menstrual cramp. And I wasn't prepared. I hadn't brought anything. Despite Mom's ultra-preparedness with the trip to the gynecologist, neither of us had thought to pack the monthly supplies. She probably figured that I wouldn't have to worry with two women in the house. There'd be plenty.

I went to the hall bathroom and looked under the cabinet. I found panty shields, like that would help. The tampons were some kind of special teen, light-flow crap. Yeah. I didn't think so.

I knocked on Caroline's door. When she yelled for me to come in, I tried to brace myself. Think of it as a bonding experience. "Um, Caroline. Are there any tampons besides the ones in the bathroom?"

Haley, I noted, was watching me with interest.

"Nope. Sorry." Caroline sat cross-legged on the bed. "Won't those work?"

I shook my head. "No." I didn't think she needed to know I bled like a stuck pig. Which I did. Lucky me. "Does your mom have anything?"

"Uh uh. She had a hysterectomy."

I guess I should have been reassured by the fact that Diane and Dad wouldn't be making any babies. Instead, I really just wanted a tampon.

"When will she be home?"

"Late," Caroline said with a shrug. "She and her friends are going to an art show, and they usually go out for drinks after."

Crap. Haley hadn't volunteered to help, but she could have a tampon hidden in her bag. She apparently didn't like me enough to enter the conversation. "Have you got anything?" I asked her.

She gave me this irritated look. "I'd have told you if I did. Besides, my periods are so light, I hardly need anything. My mother says it's because I'm underweight."

Don't scratch her eyes out, I told myself. She probably just didn't have enough estrogen to have a heavy period since she was barely human. If I snapped at Haley, I'd be insulting Caroline too. She apparently had the world's lightest periods as well. "Thanks anyway," I said.

I went the bathroom and checked the situation. I was running out of time. I grabbed Caroline's wimpy supplies for a short, very short-term solution.

I had no choice but to ask my dad to run me to the store. I couldn't even stand to watch a tampon commercial with my father in the same room, but I couldn't wait for a possibly drunk, and definitely irritating, stepmonster to drive me out in the middle of the night.

Dad had the surround sound up loud and the lights dimmed. He was soaking up Mad Men when I interrupted.

"Dad, um, have you got a minute?"

He picked up his much-loved remote and paused the show. "Sure, hon. What's up?"

"I kind of need you to take me to the store."

"What?" He blinked. "Now?"

"Yes." With a nod, I said, "I need some supplies."

He wrinkled his forehead. "Supplies? Like school supplies? On Friday night?"

I looked down at my sneakers. "Um. No. Like feminine supplies."

"Huh? Oh," Dad said finally getting it. His ears turned red. "Oh, I see. You need them now?"

"Sorry, Dad." I still couldn't look at him. Could a person actually die of mortification?

Dad stood, taking up half the basement with his height and bulk, and turned off the television. He set the remote on the edge of the recliner. "Let's get going then. Which store do you want to go to? There's a Target that's easy to get to."

"Target's good."

Dad must have been as embarrassed as I was because he babbled the whole way to the store.

"Yeah, Dad," I said in answer to his question. "I do think Target's way cooler than the other discount stores. It is nice for the lower middle class to have access to stylish clothing at a lower price." Huh?

Dad always drove with the windows down, so my hair slapped me in the face the whole way. His hair was too short to bother him, and he claimed to like the fresh air. Dad had always been the totally health conscious, outdoorsy type—eating granola, doing hours on the Nordic Trak, and going on long walks. At least pulling my hair out of my mouth kept me somewhat distracted from the horror of the whole experience. I

JULI ALEXANDER

hadn't been thinking when I'd left home, or I would have grabbed a scrunchie. We finally pulled into the lot and Dad asked if he should go in with me.

"No, thanks. I do need some money though."

"Oh, right." Dad pulled out a five.

"Um, I need at least twenty," I informed him.

"Really?" His eyes bugged a little behind his glasses.

"Yeah."

With a sigh, he pulled a fifty out of his wallet.

I snatched it before he could reconsider. Then I opened the door and climbed out.

As I walked to the door, I combed my hair out of my face and attempted to tame it.

The thing is that normally I'm a really fast shopper. I mean if I'm getting a few things for Mom at the grocery, I'm like lightning. But I so did not want anyone to see me walking around the store on a Friday night, alone, with a cart full of feminine hygiene products. I was moving at double speed.

I grabbed a shirt as I passed the women's section. The store wasn't crowded since it was almost closing time, but I didn't want to risk total exposure. Then I loaded in the jumbo box of tampons and maxipads. No use coming back next month. I threw in a jumbo-sized Advil and a bag of M&M's. Gotta have chocolate. The shirt nicely covered everything until I got to the front of the store.

This was where the whole Mission Grab the Tampons and Get Out thing went all to hell. Only one lane was open, and it was manned by a guy. A young guy. Like high school. I looked up at the ceiling. Hadn't I been going to church every day since like birth? Where was my reward? Was it too much to ask for a woman to handle my tampons?

Dad was outside waiting, and I had to have them. I had no choice. I had to brazen it out. So I pushed the cart up to the lane and handed the guy the shirt. "I changed my mind about the shirt," I said.

"Okay," he said and stuck it in the mind-changing bin.

Then I unloaded all my menstrual supplies, trained my gaze on the window, and held out the fifty.

78

I heard him gulp. Don't blush. Don't freak. He does this all the time. He doesn't know me anyway. He's probably even in college or something.

After what seemed like hours, he said, "That will be twenty nine forty seven."

He took the fifty and stuck the change in my hand. Then he loaded it all into a bag which I snatched up.

"Thanks," I mumbled. Because I did have manners after all.

I cruised through the automatic doors and ran to the car. Mom was going to call me any minute, and I was so going to let her have it.

I handed Dad the wad of change. He hated when I did that, but he didn't say a word this time. He just grumbled something about thirty dollars and pulled away from the curb.

Back at Dad's, I popped in to tell Caroline I was hitting the sack since I had cramps. She blinked like she had no idea what I was talking about. Did she not have cramps either?

I didn't end up yelling at my mother. She sounded exhausted by the time she called. She'd been flying all day.

"So," I said, putting my Meg Cabot book down on my bed. I was reading the 1-800-Where-R-You series for the second time. "Is it going okay with Donald so far?"

"Yes, Sweetie. Don't you worry." Then she told me all about the view from her apartment over the garage.

As if I believed she was really living over the garage. Puh-lease.

"Have you decided about going out for soccer yet?"

"I signed up." I didn't like looking like an idiot, and I wasn't sure I could do it. Even on the Junior Varsity of a small parochial school league. I rolled over on my back on my bed.

"I think it will be good for you, Ally. Really, what do you have to lose?"

My pride. My dignity. A few brain cells if I took a header the wrong way.

When Diane got home, she came in to check on me. "Caroline said you needed some tampons. Should I run out and get some?"

Apparently, my dad hadn't told her. You'd think he'd have the courage to discuss menstruation with his own wife but apparently not. "No thanks. Dad took me to Target. But I appreciate you asking." And I did. She could have just blown me off and gone to bed.

"Oh. Okay. I'll see you in the morning then."

"Good night," I said. Maybe I should make more of an effort to like her.

An hour later, the house was quiet. I stopped by the bathroom and took care of the necessary tasks. Then I slipped on a bra and clean shorts and t-shirt. It was too weird being outside braless, not to mention hanging out with a boy. Sure I'd done it for the first decade of my life, but that had been pre-boobs. I was only a B-cup, but they seemed pretty big and bouncy to me.

It was just after midnight when I slipped through the gate at Jonathan's. Mojo didn't even bother to greet me. When I got closer, I saw that he and Buddy were cuddled up at Jonathan's side. He was sitting on the swing. The cot, blankets, and pillows were on the patio.

"Hey," he said. "I didn't know for sure if you'd be coming."

I sat down on the cot. "It doesn't look like he needs me, does it?"

"Oh," Jonathan said in a loud whisper. "He does. Mojo just settled down. I think he knew you were on your way."

I smiled. "Thanks."

"You can sleep here again. That is..." He looked uncertain. "Was it comfortable? I figured it would be more comfortable than the cot."

"It was fine," I told him. "But I can sleep on the cot."

"No," he disentangled himself from the dogs and stood, holding the swing to minimize the swaying and creaking. "You should get to sleep with Mojo." Then he hesitated. "Unless you don't want..."

Good grief. "I'll take the swing. Thanks." I knew I should probably suggest that we rotate nights or something. That way he wouldn't have to sleep out here all the time. But I liked having him out here. I didn't want to give him an excuse to go inside, or even worse, make him think I wanted him to leave.

I moved onto the swing and he tossed me a pillow and blanket. Then he stretched out on the cot.

"Move over a little, Mojo," I said. "I can't get my feet on."

Mojo actually did what I said, but I'm pretty sure it was a fluke. I stretched out and covered up. "Where were you today?" I asked Jonathan.

"Colin had a soccer scrimmage. Me and Dave went to see him play."

"How'd they do?"

"They won. Colin's amazing. He's always been good at sports. He plays everything."

"You've known him a long time?"

"We've been friends since second grade."

"Madison and I've been friends since first. She's almost like my sister."

"Yeah," he said, sounding surprised. "Colin's like a brother."

"Maybe your brother can teach me some soccer tricks," I said. "I signed up to play JV."

"Really? That's awesome." He rolled over on his side. "I could ask Colin—"

"Oh, no. I was just kidding. I'm really not very good, and it would just embarrass me."

I couldn't see him, but I suspected he rolled his eyes. "It's just Colin."

"He may be like a brother to you, but he's a stranger to me."

"Fine. I'll let Ben show you some moves."

"Your little brother?" If I could learn something from a four-year-old, I really had no business being on the team.

"He plays."

"Um, okay."

"So it's okay for Ben but not Colin? They're both my brothers."

I threw my pillow at him and the swing squeaked in protest. "Fine. I'll do it, if you put on a skirt and let Caroline teach you some cheers." Crap! Why had I brought her up? Things were going so well.

"Not freakin' likely," he said and threw the pillow at me. Hard.

"Ow!"

"Sorry," he said. "I guess I underestimated my strength."

I was about to forgive him when he added, "I didn't hurt Buddy did I?"

"Jerk," I snapped, sending the pillow sailing back toward his face.

He laughed, loud.

"Stop," he said. "Stop it. You're going to get us busted."

"Then quit being a prick."

"Ooh. The girl's got a mouth on her. I'll stop," he said, but I could tell he was still fighting a laugh.

"Good night," I said with what I hoped was authority.

"Night," he said.

CHAPTER NINE

With makeup, sometimes less is more. Or less is less awful. —
Ally's Brutal Teen Truths

On Saturday morning, the getaway was more hectic
because his family was already stirring when the dogs woke us
up. I slipped back into bed at my house and slept til noon. It
wasn't easy sleeping outside all the time. Caroline woke me up
to inform me she was headed to the mall.

"What are you doing today?"

"I'm supposed to go over to Madison's."

"Well, get up then. The day's a'wasting."

Did she just say a'wasting? "Okay."

"I have time to do your makeup before I go," Caroline said.
"But only if you hurry and jump in the shower now."

I was interested to see what her skills could do for me.
"Going," I said climbing out of bed.

I showered and Caroline got set up in her room. You'd
think she was performing brain surgery or something as
seriously as she was taking it. She brought in two extra lamps.

My hair was still wet, but she informed me that she
couldn't wait any longer.

Then she got out all these brushes and things. I usually,
okay always, just use the cheap little brush that comes with the
blush. I mean, that's what it's for, right? Not Caroline. She had
an arsenal of application tools.

First she used toner on my face with a cotton ball. I would
have used a tissue, if I had toner. She told me how to shade to
make my nose not look so wide. Hello! My nose wasn't wide. I
had no problems with any part of my face except my eyes,

which were too small. But apparently, I had serious nose issues too. Who knew?

Thirty minutes later, I had more makeup on than Johnny Depp in Pirates of the Caribbean. I was, of course, really hoping for a different result. But when Caroline finally let me have the mirror, I realized I'd been hoping for too much. I didn't look better. Just different, and not a little slutty, I must say. My complexion didn't look right. And my eyes looked even smaller.

"Well, what do you think?" She chewed on her lip waiting for my answer.

"It's great. I...love it. Thanks."

"Do you really? I wasn't sure."

Okay, even Caroline knew I didn't look good.

"I've got to go, but we can do it again anytime. I'll show you how to get the eye shadow to do right, too."

"Thanks, Caroline," I said, trying to hide my depression over the sad state of my ugliness. I'd been really hoping she could make me look prettier. This wasn't prettier.

When I got to Madison's house, she said, "What the hell? Did somebody's makeup kit explode on your face?"

"Sort of," I said, wondering why I didn't have friends with more sensitivity.

"Hi, Ally," her mother called from the kitchen. "Oh." She stopped and studied me. "New look?"

"I know it's terrible. My stepsister was trying to help. I guess I'm just hopeless."

Madison's mom was freaking me out the way she was staring. Finally she said, "Not hopeless. Those are just all the wrong tones for you. You don't need to be wearing browns. And the foundation is too light. Your stepsister must have used her own makeup."

I nodded.

"Tell you what girls." Madison's mother must have felt sorry for me what with my mom abandoning me and all. "I'll call in an expert. My Mary Kay consultant works wonders. Let me see if she can get here this afternoon."

"Oh, you don't have to— " I didn't mean to ruin the whole day.

"No. Let her," Madison said. "She's been promising me for weeks and hasn't done it yet."

But she didn't meet my eyes, and I figured she was just trying to make me feel better.

"Oh, definitely," Suzanne, the big-haired, make-up consultant said later. "Browns or purples would just wash you out. You'd look sickly."

"So what does that leave?" Madison asked.

"Greens, blues, and pinks," Suzanne answered. "Done right, they'll be perfect."

I winced. I was pretty sure she was going to turn me into something out of the 1980's with tons of blue eyeshadow. Hey, I'd seen pictures. The 80's weren't as ugly as the 70's, but they weren't pretty either.

You can imagine my shock when Suzanne finished and handed me the mirror. And I looked pretty good. Better than usual. Not as good as Caroline on a bad day. But decent. Somehow she'd used the eye makeup to make my eyes look bigger instead of emphasizing their small size like Caroline had.

Madison looked good too in her purples.

Madison's mom had this expression of pure joy on her face. I guess make-up was something of a religious experience for her. She was so excited that she bought us each the skin care kit, plus eyeshadow, eyeliner, lipsticks, blush, and powder. She didn't think either one of us needed foundation and Suzanne couldn't budge her.

"Mrs. Hudson," I said. "You really don't have to buy me all this."

"Consider it a birthday present," she said.

"My birthday isn't until February."

"Then I'm way ahead of schedule for once." She smiled at me.

"Thank you."

We were all happy when Madison's mom dropped me off. Especially Suzanne who must have made a fortune.

I glanced at the clouds in the sky before going inside. Surely it wouldn't rain.

Caroline and Haley were hanging in her room.

"How was the mall?" I asked.

Haley rolled her eyes. "She didn't tell me we were meeting Liam there."

Caroline grinned. Then she noticed my makeup. "Hey. What did you do?"

"Madison's mom decided to have a makeup party." I held up my bag. "She bought me all kinds of stuff."

"It looks really good on you," Caroline said.

"Thanks." I didn't want her to think I didn't appreciate her help earlier. I mean, I know she meant well. "Maybe you can help me put it on tomorrow."

She smiled. "Sure!"

"Haley, you don't like Liam?" I asked as her comment finally registered.

"Oh, he's okay. But he showed up alone. Without any friends." With a glare at Caroline, she said, "I was like the eighth wheel or something." Her lips were always pressed into a pout.

"Third," Caroline said. "And you weren't."

"She owes me," Haley said raising her eyebrow at me. — Yikes! I wouldn't want to owe that girl anything.

The rain was coming down in sheets by the time we ate dinner. I twirled the spaghetti on my fork and tried to decide what to do about Mojo. I couldn't sleep out in the rain. Unless Jonathan had a tent. No, that would be ridiculous. Plus we wouldn't hear anybody coming with the noise from the rain. And the dogs would be wet and muddy anyway.

As soon as Haley, Caroline, and Diane finished their dinner, I dashed next door with the beat-up black umbrella Diane kept in the foyer.

The tropical rainstorm nearly blew me away as I stood at Jonathan's front door. I rang the bell.

He answered immediately. "I thought you might come over." He stepped back and motioned me in.

I dumped the ratty umbrella on his stoop and stepped inside. Unfortunately a gust of wind snagged the umbrella. I wasn't paying attention, but Jonathan rushed out to catch it.

The soggy black mass dripped on the floor when he brought it in. His hair and shoulders were wet.

"Thanks," I said. "You shouldn't have sacrificed yourself."

He shut the door, sending some more water flying. "No problem."

"I came to check with you about the dogs."

With a nod, he set the umbrella on the doormat. "I knew you'd be worried. I got permission from my dad to let them both sleep with me for this one night. He has a soft spot when it comes to thunderstorms."

Thank goodness! "That's great. I was worried."

"We were just eating dinner, but you could stay for a while."

I turned to see Jonathan's mother, father, and little brother staring at me from the dining table. Their interested gazes freaked me out. "Um, no, I think I need to go." I waved in their direction, picked up my umbrella, and opened the door. "Thanks, though," I said to Jonathan before dashing back out into the rain.

Since soccer practice officially started on Monday, I went to Madison's on Sunday to work with her and MC. It was actually fun kicking the ball around with them even in the muddy, slushy grass. Then, we hit the pool.

"So what's the word from your mom?" MC asked as we drifted on the rafts.

I didn't really feel like talking about my mom. "She called last night. She's fine. No big deal."

"I still can't believe she really left," Madison said. "I never would have pictured her moving across the country."

"For a guy," MC added.

I hadn't shown them the website. I guess I didn't want them to think my mother was a total loser.

"When are you going to meet him?" Madison asked.

Good question. I shrugged. "She hasn't said anything about it. I guess not until she's sure she really likes him." I decided to throw them a bone. I told them about the tampon run.

MC thought it was uproariously funny. "I wish I could have seen your dad's face."

"My dad probably would freak too," Madison admitted. "Even if he is a doctor."

For some reason I couldn't understand, I didn't want to tell them about Jonathan.

When I got back to Dad's, Diane said he'd just come by. I walked over to find him in the backyard with Ben. Ben was wearing full soccer get-up. I couldn't help but grin at the little guy. His back yard had mostly dried up, but the dogs still sported muddy coats.

"Where've you been?" Ben demanded in a huff. "We were waiting."

"Sorry, Ben. I didn't know."

Jonathan nodded to the orange cones he'd set up. "I told Ben you wanted to play."

He was really too funny. "I'd love to," I told my four-year-old opponent. "Does Jonathan think he's too grown up and important to play with you?"

Jonathan glared.

"No," said Ben missing the undertones. "He's playing too." His tiny little legs were covered in blue socks and pint-sized shin guards.

"Me and Ben against you," Jonathan said with a huge smile. "Unless you think we're too much for you."

"Bring it on," I said.

I was prepared to back off of Ben and play aggressively when Jonathan had the ball. What I wasn't prepared for was Buddy. He stole the ball from me and ran off with it in his mouth.

Mojo and Ben chased after him.

"How can he get his mouth around that thing? It's bigger than his head."

"Practice," Jonathan answered. "Soccer is his favorite game."

"I'm surprised you didn't offer him as my tutor."

A mischievous glint lit his eyes. "What do you think this was all about?"

"Well," I said trying to sound irate. "I've had plenty of practice today anyway. No thanks to you."

After twenty minutes, Ben gave up chasing the dogs and flopped down in the grass beside us. He looked so disappointed.

"Wanna shoot some hoops?" Jonathan asked his brother.

"Yeah!" Ben looked at me. "Will you come?"

"Sure, but I stink."

"That's okay," Ben said, his little chest puffing out with pride. "I'll help you."

The goal was way too high for Ben, but he seemed to enjoy trying to get the ball in.

"I'm surprised you don't have another goal his size," I said to Jonathan.

"We did," he told me as he took another shot and watched Ben run to rebound it. "He refused to use it. He likes this one."

Ben caught up with the ball and brought it back in front of the goal. He leaned down, pulled the ball back between his knees, and chucked it up to the goal with as much force as he could manage. It wasn't enough. The ball hit the bottom of the rim and rocketed back at him.

Jonathan reached out with a strong arm and snagged it before it could squash his brother. A warm sensation flooded my chest. He was just too adorable.

Jonathan handed the ball to me, and I took a halfhearted shot. Ben shook his head as I missed yet again. "You aren't doing it right."

"Ben," Jonathan warned, rebounding the ball. "She's doing as well as you are."

Ben put his little hands on his hips. "Hello," he said. "I'm four."

I cracked up. His exasperated look mirrored his brother's.

"Watch how Jonathan shoots it," Ben said.

Jonathan blushed as I turned to watch him. I'd been actively avoiding focusing on him so far. I was afraid I wouldn't be able to stop watching him. Then I'd die of mortification when he noticed me drinking in his hotness.

"I've been trying to teach Ben the technique, but since the goal is nowhere near his size..." Jonathan released another perfect shot, his arm fully extended and his wrist seeming to swish down as the ball hit the net.

"It's all about the follow through," Ben said like a pro.

"I see that," I said, pulling my eyes away from Jonathan's muscular arms. Did he lift weights or something? I always thought basketball players had skinny arms.

Jonathan caught me looking at his arms, so I made this lame shooting motion to cover.

I'm pretty sure I looked like a total spaz.

"Uh," Jonathan said. "Close."

Ben just laughed. Then, he got the ball and took another granny shot.

"I'm much better at soccer," I mumbled.

The swing had dried out pretty well when I sneaked next door on Sunday night. The dogs had managed to stay damp, and pretty smelly.

"I think you got the better deal tonight," I said to Jonathan after we talked for a while.

"What do you mean?"

I motioned to the dogs next to me on the swing. "I'll probably sport eau de wet dog for the next week."

"Nothing a few dozen showers won't take care of," he said.

"They'll probably start calling me stinky."

He thought that was hilarious.

Getting teased by this guy was something I was so getting used to.

I hadn't told him about my ugly stepsister thing, but I had talked to him about Diane. He totally sided with me on the whole righteous anger thing.

"I still can't believe they had an affair when your dad was married to your mom."

"Yeah." I'd lived it. I believed it all right.

"I don't know what I'd do if my dad did that."

"Your dad won't do that."

"God, I hope not," was all he said.

Now he knew some of my dark secrets, and I knew that his mother had miscarried twice before having Ben. Apparently, Jonathan had some familiarity with the whole depressed mother situation. He said he understood why I wasn't mad at my mom for going to Seattle, but he still thought it sucked.

I agreed totally. It did suck.

As I lay there listening to the frogs, I realized that Jonathan knew more about me than even Madison and MC. I'm sure he hadn't talked to his friends much about his mother's depression either. It was nice, I thought, pulling up my covers, to have someone to talk to.

Our morning routine went pretty smoothly on Monday. I headed straight for the shower again and gave Caroline her time in the bathroom. Diane made oatmeal with raisins and honey. It wasn't bad.

When we climbed into the Range Rover, Diane had a cup of coffee, and Caroline and I each had a can of Diet Coke. None of us were morning people, so it was a quiet, peaceful ride.

I dragged my bag of soccer gear into the school and with some serious pounding, fit it into my locker. My nerves were already on edge over the idea of playing on a team. Mostly, I just felt out of sorts. Nothing seemed real today. I had a big secret that I hadn't shared with anyone, and after my nighttime talks with Jonathan, the real world seemed dull, like one big long commercial when I was waiting for my favorite show to come back on.

I was in way over my head. I ran down the field dribbling the soccer ball in front of me, too far away according to the coach. A couple of the girls were amazing. MC looked pretty good too. Madison fit in just fine. Katelyn, from French class, could dribble around any of us.

No one had told me the coach had been in the Marines, but the way she was pushing us, I knew she'd been in some branch of the armed forces. She was relentless.

Finally, we scrimmaged. I was tense and miserable because I hadn't kept a ball from going out. And then it happened. This nerdy sophomore Monique who I recognized from grade school came up and kicked the crap out of my shin. She didn't come anywhere near the ball. She was a total spaz. And just like that, I relaxed. I mean, how hard could it be to do better than Monique. After that, I started to have fun, despite the sweat and the pain in my side.

Worn out from practice, I fell asleep waiting for the house to quiet down. I woke up at one and realized I'd ditched Jonathan and Mojo. When I got over there, Jonathan was asleep on the swing with the dogs. Jonathan kept snoring softly and the dogs just raised their heads to acknowledge me soundlessly. The cot was set up next to the swing. I petted Mojo and Buddy, climbed on the cot, and fell back asleep.

When I woke, it was light, and Jonathan was gently shaking me. "Ally, it's morning."

God, my whole body was tired. "Ugh."

"No really, Ally. You have to wake up."

I opened my eyes and sat up, propping my head in my hands. "I'm up."

"I didn't think you were coming last night," Jonathan said.

He actually sounded like he'd missed me. "Sorry. Soccer wore me out, and I fell asleep."

"You'd better get going. I'll stash the blankets."

I stood and stretched. "I'll be on time tonight."

"Congratulations on soccer," he said.

"Thanks, Jonathan. I have practice again tonight. I'll come check on Mojo after dinner."

"I'll be here."

In French class on Tuesday, the principal came and got Mrs. Day. She whispered something to her and she ran out of the room.

"I'll be back in a few minutes," Mrs. Moyers said. "You may talk quietly. Mrs. Day has a family emergency."

Then she walked out and left us alone. As if we weren't going to cause trouble.

Everyone started talking at once.

I was just grateful that I had someone to talk to.

Katelyn said from the seat behind me, "I hope it's not anything too bad."

I turned around. She had the most beautiful skin. Like mocha or something. "Me too. I like Mrs. Day." Oops. I broke that never like a teacher rule. "So far."

Katelyn just nodded like I hadn't committed a huge faux pas. "Me too."

"You went to St. Luke?" I asked.

"Yeah."

"I went to St. Catherine's."

"I like high school much better."

"Me too."

"Do you live over by St. Catherine's?"

"Yes," I said without thinking. "Usually. Right now I'm living with my dad on the other side of town. Middleton Heights."

"That's down the street from my subdivision."

Five minutes later, the principal came back. By then, Katelyn and I had exchanged cell numbers and agreed to ask our parents about carpooling. She said her mother was dying to find someone to share the driving, and I figured Diane wouldn't mind getting rid of me half the time.

I'd thought playing soccer with MC and Madison would give us some time together. So far, we were too busy running our guts out to do any talking.

Coach Borkman made us all take a turn in goal. I jogged over to her, trying to catch my breath enough to talk. "Listen, Coach." Wheeze, wheeze. "I really have to tell you that I can't catch. Anything. Ever."

She just looked at me.

"No. Really. Like if someone throws me something, it hits the ground every time."

"Thanks for the heads up, Ally. You can still give it a try."

After watching me clap my hands like a seal while the ball bounced off my chest, she pulled me out of goal. "You weren't kidding," she said with amazement. "It's a good thing you're pretty good on defense."

I couldn't believe it. I was pretty good. Me? On defense? I thought back over the practice. There were fifteen of us now, and I was better than at least six of them. Oh my God! I was actually going to be playing in the games. No way.

MC didn't seem surprised when I shared this later on the phone. "Duh. Of course you will."

"I guess I just thought I'd be warming the bench."

"You've got way too much competition for the bench. Monique kicked the hell out of my shin today. I've already got a giant blue knot. The girl's a menace."

"Yeah, she really is."

"Nice job in goal by the way."

"Shut up! You know I can't catch. I warned Coach Borkman."

MC giggled. "It's hard to believe until you really see it."

"Are we really going to go there?" I threatened. I knew all her secrets, but she got cranky when I mentioned them so I gave her one last warning.

She stopped laughing. "No. Sorry. Ma'am."

The peeing in a cracked bucket incident of seventh grade would stay buried. For now. "I'm glad we could come to an understanding," I said. "Now tell me what happened in Spanish today."

I'd really missed out by taking French. MC had some of the school hotties in her Spanish class. Plus a lot of the troublemakers, so she never knew what was going to happen next. Most of them were juniors who'd put off taking a language as long as possible. "What is it," MC asked, "about bad boys that is so attractive?"

"Beats me." I didn't find bad boys appealing at all. Jonathan was way more my speed. A nice guy, who happened to be really cute. Not that I actually had a chance with him, but if I were going to have a crush, it would be on him.

I talked to my mother next. She sounded pretty good.

"The law firm is great, Ally. They had a hard time filling this position, and they are so grateful to have me. Anything I do pleases them. It's a nice change from Haynes and Hester."

"Good, Mom. Soccer's kind of like that for me. Some of the others are so bad, it doesn't matter that I'm not great. They make me look good."

"Oh, Ally, I'm so proud of you for trying out."

She was getting too gushy. "It wasn't really a try out. We all made it."

"You know what I mean. I'm proud of you for taking the chance, especially with all the changes you're having to deal with. Speaking of which, how's Mojo?"

"He's okay." I wasn't going to tell her I'd been sleeping with him. "He seems to like Buddy and Jonathan."

"And is Mojo the only one who likes Jonathan?"

"Mo-om," I said.

"No really, Ally. He seemed like a nice boy. He'd make a good boyfriend for you."

"Mom, I know you're wrapped up in your own life and all, but you have met Caroline, right?"

"Sure. Why?"

I probably wouldn't have said this to her face, but it was easier over the phone. Didn't she get it? "No boy is going to think twice about me with Caroline around."

Mom gasped. Actually gasped. "That's not true, Ally."

"You're my mother, you have to say these things. But the truth is that Caroline is beautiful. Jonathan would be crazy to like me with her around."

Mom didn't answer for a minute. "I didn't realize you felt that way. You should have told me. I thought Caroline was nice to you."

"She is, but that doesn't change the facts."

"Ally," Mom said, "I want you to listen and listen good. You are a pretty girl and any guy would be lucky to go out with you. You may think Caroline is prettier, but that doesn't mean other people think so."

"She modeled, Mom!"

"Okay, fine. Are there boys at your school who are cuter than Jonathan?"

"Yeah." I guess based on looks alone.

"Picture Jonathan standing with a group of these guys. Now be honest with yourself, Ally. Wouldn't you still be interested in Jonathan?"

I thought for a minute. One of the varsity soccer players looked like a young Brad Pitt. And that Liam guy Caroline liked was almost pretty, he was so handsome. She was actually right. I wouldn't have believed it. "I would still be more interested in Jonathan than the others," I admitted. Could it possibly be true? Could he notice me despite Caroline?

"I've got to get back to work, Ally," Mom said. It was after dinner in Charlotte, but she was still at work. This whole time difference thing was messing with me. "I'll call you later."

"Okay, Mom. Thanks."

"I love you."

"I love you, too."

Diane loved the idea of carpooling. "And I think it's great you've got an African-American friend now. That was one thing I told Ted about the Catholic schools. They don't have enough diversity." She tried so hard to be politically correct that she missed the boat entirely.

I was so sure that Diane didn't have any ulterior motives for me going to public school. Like a lot more money for art classes on drawing vaginas with charcoal.

She did call Katelyn's mom, and they arranged to start on Monday.

I thought Katelyn was pretty cool. Avoiding an hour every day in the car with Diane, even cooler.

I went to my room and checked in with Katelyn. She was psyched too. "Now when you meet Diane," I said, "remember that she's only my stepmother. She's not a blood relation or anything." I hoped she wouldn't start babbling about diversity again. How embarrassing.

My French homework took some time. I had to listen to the CD and do a computer exercise. Finally, I got everything done. The house was quiet, so I slipped out.

I had just settled in with Mojo and Buddy when my cell rang. Mom. I answered quickly in a whisper.

"Ally, are you still up? I was just going to leave you a message. I'll be in court tomorrow, and I may not be able to talk."

Mom runs the power point presentation while the lawyer argues the case. "It's okay, Mom."

"How's everything going?"

"Fine," I said with a glance at Jonathan. Please don't let the dogs bark.

"The connection sounds funny," she said.

Yeah. Because I was outside in frog world. "Sounds fine to me, Mom."

"Well, it's late, so I won't keep you."

"Love you, Mom."

"Love you too, Ally."

After I ended the call, Jonathan raised a brow. "That was close."

"Oh, she'd be totally cool with this." I started laughing before I could finish. She so would not be okay with it.

"How's she doing?"

"Okay, I guess."

"And Diane?"

"I guess things aren't so bad." I told him about Katelyn and carpooling.

"Maybe you should have just transferred to Plum."

"No way. I don't want to change schools. And I wouldn't want to go to the same school as Caroline."

"Why not?" he asked.

Because she's beautiful and I am not. "It would just be weird," I said.

"I guess it would be crazy to transfer now, when you may have to change schools again in January."

I didn't say anything.

"Sorry," he said. "I didn't mean to bring that up."

"Let's just pretend my mother isn't going to yank me out of North Carolina in a few months."

"Maybe she isn't."

"Good."

"No," he said. "Maybe she really won't."

"So how's b-ball," I said firmly.

He got the message. "Great. How's soccer?"

"Better. I'm glad I did it."

"Do I get to come to a game?"

I had no idea what to say. "Sure. If you want." I doubted I could even focus on the game with him there. "But nobody can come to the first one. I have enough to worry about."

"Cool," he said. "I'll plan on the second one."

He wouldn't really come. Would he? He had better things to do.

Three teachers busted me for daydreaming on Wednesday. I felt like a total idiot. After each class, I went up and apologized. I know, total suck-up move, but I couldn't have my teachers mad at me the first week of school. When I carefully explained that I'd run out of my prescription antihistamine and had taken one of my Dad's, they all nodded in sympathy. Allergies were the universal language in the Southeast.

Diane picked me up after she'd already run Caroline home. I started thinking about Jonathan again, and the next thing I knew, we were home. I was starting to think I had a problem. Could I be addicted to the guy? I hated having crushes, but I couldn't seem to nip this one in the bud.

"Oh, Ally," Diane said as we walked into the house. "You might be interested in this. I'm doing a project with polymer clay. I taped a few shows on how to do it, and I bought plenty of supplies. Do you want to make something with me?"

Okay, polymer clay is bright and happy. MC's oldest sister makes jewelry for her all the time that I love. Polymer clay actually sounded like something I would be willing to spend time with Diane to do.

"Look in the bag," she said, on her way down the hall. "I got forty different colors."

I walked over to the counter, and saw the receipt at the top of the bag. She'd spent two hundred and twenty-seven dollars on clay. I was going to end up in plumbing school if she kept this up.

Diane came back in. "So what do you think?"

"It looks like fun," I told her, careful to keep the bitterness from my tone. "But I've got loads of homework. Maybe next time."

"Okay," Diane said, barely sparing me a glance as she walked over to the counter and started sorting through her purchases.

Caroline and I settled in on the sofas downstairs and cranked through our homework. We had the television on in the background, reruns of *That Seventies Show*. If those guys weren't a reason to study and go to college, I don't know what was.

We watched prime time TV together and then both crawled off to bed. Caroline said her thighs were burning from all the cheering. I told her no way were they worse than mine.

When I got over to Jonathan's at midnight, he wasn't out yet. I petted the dogs and climbed onto the swing. By now, I had the hand of steadying it so it wouldn't creak so much.

He finally slipped out the door thirty minutes later.

"Sorry," he said in a low voice. "I had a paper that was kicking my butt."

"That sucks," I said. I'd always thought of public school as lightweight. "What was it in?"

"AP American Government."

"You're taking an Advanced Placement class as a freshman?"

"Yeah. Just that one. It's a long story, but my dad found out about this internship thing at the courthouse next summer. To qualify, I'd have to have this class."

"What would you do at the courthouse?"

"I'm not really sure." He handed me a blanket and rushed off to get the cot.

When he got back, he said, "Dad's just real psyched about it. And it does sound interesting."

"Is the class hard?"

"Nah. It's just going to be a lot of work."

I didn't think I'd want to go into politics or anything. I tried to picture myself as a lawyer or a judge, and the image just didn't come.

"Do you get credit for the internship?" I asked.

He didn't answer and when I leaned up to get a good look at him, he was sound asleep.

He looked even more like his little brother when he was sleeping peacefully. I brought my head back down on my pillow and stared up at the stars until I drifted off.

Thursday night, my whole body ached. Four straight days of soccer practice had almost done me in. To be honest, sleeping on that crappy swing probably wasn't helping either. But I wasn't trading that for anything.

Jonathan and I were actually friends. We talked to each other. About important stuff. This morning, we'd been finishing each other's sentences as we scrambled to put away the cot and blankets. I had high hopes that he saw me as more than a friend. I had caught him looking at me kind of funny. Besides, Liam and Caroline were a hot item now, so if he'd been interested in her...Just maybe he wasn't anymore.

Despite the fact that my legs hurt with every step I took, I made my way over to Jonathan's when everyone had gone to sleep.

I caught myself grinning whenever I thought about him. Basically, I had it bad. If he didn't like me back, I was going to be devastated.

I crossed the dark yard to see my three boys, well the two dogs and Jonathan, chilling on the swing. As usual, he'd set up the cot.

"Hey," he whispered.

"Hey," I whispered back. Tonight felt different for some reason. Special.

He got up and I sat on the swing. We'd long ago stopped arguing over it. He sat on the cot which was pulled so close to the swing, it was practically one big bed. "I missed you today," he said so softly I had to strain to hear it.

"You did?"

"Yes." Then, he did something unbelievable. He reached out and touched my cheek. Then, he leaned in and touched his lips to mine.

Oh God! I had been waiting for this for fourteen years, and it was finally here. My first real kiss. And it was wonderful. I put my hands on his shoulders and tried to kiss him back, but a loud squeak pierced the air.

We both froze.

"The swing," he whispered.

We sat there for a moment with our arms around each other waiting for his parents.

They didn't come.

"Try getting up really slowly," he suggested, "and sitting on the cot with me."

"Okay."

I climbed off the swing without any more trouble. Except that when I stood up, so did Mojo and Buddy. They started jumping around and bumping into the cot and getting all excited.

"No, Mojo."

"Sit," Jonathan ordered.

The dogs ignored us. They decided it was time to play and headed across the yard. Then they started barking.

Crap!

Jonathan blanched. "Get back on the swing."

I scrambled to obey. I didn't see any alternative.

Jonathan climbed on the cot and stretched out. "Buddy," he whispered. "Here boy."

The dogs, seeing that we'd returned to bed, decided to call it a night. They piled in with me, the swing creaking as they did so.

"Stupid dogs," Jonathan muttered.

"They're like chaperones or something," I said trying not to laugh.

Jonathan reached out and took my hand in his. "Tomorrow morning," he said. "I'm kissing you."

Elated, I answered, "You'd better."

We fell asleep holding hands.

When I woke up, the dogs were going ballistic, and Jonathan was muttering something about, "Leave the joggers alone, Buddy."

I smiled at Jonathan's sleeping face next to me and squeezed his hand.

Then I realized we were not alone. The dogs weren't barking at a jogger. They were barking at an intruder. Sadly, not a serial killer. Worse. Way worse.

CHAPTER TEN

Dads are generally oblivious, but God help you if they ever start paying attention. -Ally's Brutal Teen Truths

A tall form was standing over my head, and I looked up to see my dad, his face red with fury.

"Allison Margaret Wright."

I jumped and released Jonathan's hand. He was a split second behind me, jumping to his feet, and sputtering to my father that it wasn't what it looked like.

My dad didn't bother to be polite to Jonathan. He just said in this menacing tone, "I will deal with you later." Then he turned to me. "Ally, get your butt inside."

I got my butt inside. I ran as fast as I could back to Dad's house.

Diane was standing in the kitchen pouring some orange juice. She was wearing a robe, and honestly she looked like hell. She must have forgotten her makeup this morning.

My eyes darted toward the hall, but I knew I couldn't hide in my room. Once I explained, Dad would probably be reasonable. Yeah, right.

I stalked across the kitchen tiles to the table and pulled out a chair, which sent a noise of protest as it scraped against the floor. Dad stormed in milliseconds later, and a quick calculation told me that he hadn't had enough time to do Jonathan bodily harm.

He slammed the front door so hard the paintings in the foyer rattled and the crooked pots danced over the stove.

Diane gave me a wide-eyed look revealing blood-shot eyes.

Before she could say anything, Dad said, "Diane, I need a moment with my daughter, please."

My dad rarely lost his temper. Diane gulped, picked up her glass of juice, and left the room.

My dad walked over to the table, crossed his arms, and said in a menacing voice, "Now would you like to tell me why I found my fourteen-year-old daughter sleeping with a boy at the neighbor's house?"

My mind raced with possible approaches to defuse his anger. I didn't come up with anything that might work. Dad was furious. "I was trying to help Mojo."

Dad raised a brow. "Mojo?"

"He was, um, barking a lot." I kept my eyes on my fingernails. "So I went over there to quiet him down. He gets upset when I leave, and I didn't want him to wake the whole neighborhood."

"Diane told me he was doing fine. I haven't heard him barking much at all."

"Well," I gulped and risked a glance at him. "Yeah. Because I've been going over there."

This throbbing vein suddenly appeared on Dad's forehead. I'd never noticed it before.

"Are you telling me that you've been sleeping over there every night?"

Oh, crap. I probably shouldn't have shared that piece of information. "Yes," I squeaked. "But it wasn't anything bad, Dad. I was just keeping Mojo quiet."

Through his clenched jaw, he asked, "And why was the boy there?"

Hmm. That wasn't so easy to explain. "Well. I guess he felt sorry for me, so he slept on the cot." Yeah, it wasn't sounding so good.

"That doesn't make any sense at all."

"Well, um, I guess he was trying to help me keep his parents from noticing. I didn't want to cause any trouble."

"You didn't want to cause any trouble." Dad's vein throbbed. "Well, missy, you've got plenty of trouble now."

See, I had already figured that part out for myself. I'm pretty clever that way.

JULI ALEXANDER

"I don't even know where to start. No. I do. Go to your room," Dad ordered, pointing with a violent motion toward my room. "Now!"

I went. I heard Dad talking to Diane in the kitchen. Caroline came in, sleepy-eyed. "What's going on? Are you okay? Is Ted yelling?"

I sat on the bed hugging my pillow to my chest. "Big mess. Not okay. Yes, he's yelling."

Caroline was immediately fully alert. She came in and shut the door. "Do tell."

So, I told her. About the dogs and the nighttime talks and the sleeping outside.

She clapped her hands together. "Oh my God, Ally. Are you dating him?"

"No." I shook my head. She was getting the wrong idea. "I don't know if he really likes me. Except as a friend."

"Did he kiss you?" Her face brightened at the juicy gossip.

"Well, yeah, but it was the middle of the night. It was like we weren't really us, you know. Like magical sort of."

"He likes you." She grinned and sat on the bed bouncing with excitement.

She didn't ask if I liked him. I guess it was pretty obvious. "I guess it doesn't matter now anyway. I'll never be allowed to leave my room again."

"Sure you will," Caroline said. "I'll offer to keep an eye on you. That way I can close my eyes at just the right moments."

"Dad won't go for that. And I don't know if there will be any more moments."

"He can't watch you all day and all night. He's gone most of the time. Trust me. He'll calm down."

"Poor Mojo," I said.

I showered and dressed for school, which wasn't easy with my mind flying in a million directions at once. Jonathan kissed me. His beautiful face, the feel of his hands, Dad's horror.

Finally, Dad delivered the verdict. He pointed for me to sit on the living room couch. He stood, towering over me as I glanced at the easel and the craft table. I'd never sat in here before.

"You will not go next door unless Caroline or Diane accompany you. Mojo will spend the days over there, and at night, he can sleep with you in the family room downstairs."

Before I could comprehend it, he added, "And we're installing an alarm system. There will be no more sneaking out."

At least he wasn't locking me in the house. "But...What about Diane's allergies."

Dad just gave me this exasperated look. "I guess she'll double her antihistamines."

Later, I realized what he really meant. Diane's allergies trumped my dog. But my virginity trumped her allergies. Score one for me.

"Wow," Diane said Friday evening while we waited for dad to get back from the grocery. We were grilling out. "I think he even did a search for chastity belts on the Internet."

Caroline laughed from across the kitchen table. "They don't make those anymore. Those were like medieval, right?"

"Nothing happened," I said, sipping at my green tea. I was too downtrodden to argue when Diane handed it to me. As if my virginity were actually in danger. It had taken me fourteen years to get a real kiss. Plus, I had a pact with my friends. We weren't having sex until we were at least eighteen. Yeah, the traditional catholic teaching was to wait until marriage, but we'd made some modifications. Eighteen seemed entirely reasonable. We weren't going to end up pregnant teenagers. MC had an aunt who'd gone that route, and it hadn't turned out well.

I'd learned that my dad had gotten a flight in the wee hours of the morning. He'd come in from the airport and checked on all of us. I wasn't in my bed. Then at school, I'd been busted for passing notes in class, saved from total social ruin only by the cryptic nature of my conversation with Madison.

"I thought you were going out with your friends tonight, Caroline," Diane said.

Caroline glanced at me. "I canceled. I thought you guys might need me around here."

She'd ditched her friends to help me out? Wow. I was truly touched. "Thanks, Caroline."

"Ted is wigging out pretty bad," Diane said. "He did an extra two hours on the Nordic Track. I think the part that really got him was that you were holding hands while you slept."

"What?" Caroline squealed. "You didn't tell me that part. That's even bigger than the kiss!"

I glanced at Diane, but Caroline waved away my concern. "She knows you kissed him. How could you not?"

Great. I grimaced.

"Besides, Ally. This is huge. Holding hands in the mall is one thing. In a movie is a bigger deal. But at night while you sleep! That's way intimate. He so likes you."

The heat rose in my cheeks. It was hard enough discussing this with Caroline, but with Diane too. No thanks.

Fortunately, there hadn't been anyone home next door when Caroline and I went over to play with Buddy after school. I wasn't ready to face Jonathan yet. Much less his parents. And with someone, Caroline of all people, watching? It would make me way too nervous. But I was desperate to know what my dad had said to them. I'd been miserable all day that I'd gotten Jonathan in trouble.

The JV football team at Plum didn't start games until next week. That meant this was Caroline's last free Friday night and she'd given it up for me. Were we actually friends?

"What time am I supposed to bring Mojo over?" I asked Diane.

"As late as possible. Right before bed on school nights, and then on weekends, whenever you're serious about going to sleep."

She sounded resigned to the whole thing. I guess my father had put his foot down.

"I'll sleep downstairs with you tonight," Caroline said. "To babysit you so you don't sneak out." From her tone, she was kidding.

"Can you have some friends over tomorrow night, Ally?" Diane asked. "I think your father would find that reassuring. Caroline is spending the night at Haley's."

"Sure. MC or Madison would come."

"Invite them both," Diane suggested. "It will distract your father."

I wasn't going to argue. "I'll go call them."

I'd never seen my dad standing so stiffly at the grill. Usually cooking steaks made him Mr. Happy Guy. Not today. He did appear to have calmed down some, but he wasn't back to normal by any means.

"I'd like to talk to you after dinner, Ally," he said when I brought him a plate for the steaks. "In private."

I pasted a smile on my face. "Sure thing, Dad." This could not be good. I slid a look at Caroline.

She grimaced.

As I walked past her, I whispered, "Pray for me."

She giggled.

"No, I mean it," I hissed with a glance at Dad.

"Oh, come on. How bad could it be?"

Mojo and Buddy barked excitedly about the smell of meat in the air. They were standing in the middle of Jonathan's yard watching us. Dad didn't seem to even notice them.

Dad served up the steaks and removed his Grillmaster apron to sit at the table with us. Diane had cut up some fresh tomatoes and baked some potatoes.

Diane and Caroline tried to keep up the conversation during dinner, but Dad and I were no help. Finally, he pushed back his chair and nodded in my direction.

I followed Dad down to his office. He sat behind the desk and pointed to the chair. I sat. I felt like I was being interrogated by the FBI. The only thing missing was the bare lightbulb and whatever torture devices. Dads didn't need torture devices. They already had you in their clutches. Plus, they could always use the disappointment card to manipulate you. Suspects had all kinds of rights. Teenage daughters, not so much.

Dad kept me squirming for a few minutes by just staring at me with this resigned expression.

Finally, he said, "Your mother assured me that she had taken care of discussing s—" he sputtered but couldn't quite get the word out, "the birds and the bees."

"She did. She has. Everything's fine. We don't need to have a talk." My assurances didn't seem to help.

"The thing is Ally, I know you are more comfortable talking about these things with your mother." There was that vein again.

"Yes." If I could just head him off...

"Unfortunately, your mother has never been a teenage boy. And I have. I think it would be remiss of me if I didn't share with you exactly what goes through the mind of a teenage boy."

Oh. No! I didn't want to be privy to any thoughts my dad had ever had on this particular subject. "It's really not necessary—"

"It is necessary, Ally," he said in a firm tone. "In fact, I shouldn't have waited this long. You see, teenage boys are base sex hounds with nothing on their minds besides getting into a girl's panties."

My jaw dropped. Dads should never say "sex hounds" or "panties." Ever.

How could I make it stop? "Dad, it was innocent really."

He held up a hand. "It's never innocent, Ally. Boys cannot be trusted. They will say whatever they think you want to hear. They are completely controlled by hormones, and honestly almost incapable of any sort of rational thought when a girl is around. Teenage boys have no redeeming values whatsoever."

Now he had to be exaggerating.

But the lecture was just beginning, and thirty minutes later I stumbled from the room in a daze. Pregnancy, disease, lies... Boys were apparently the antichrist. What would he have said if I'd been a boy? Or if I had a brother?

One thing was for sure. I was really lucky those chastity belts weren't around anymore.

Caroline was sitting on my bed when I got upstairs.

"Did you survive?" she asked.

I just nodded. "It was a close call." I shut my door and sat at my desk. "Does your father give you lectures on how teenage boys are the spawn of Satan?"

The corner of her lip quirked. "Not exactly. I don't think he'd say that because of my stepbrothers. But he has given me the whole, 'boys only want one thing' lecture."

"Do our fathers think we're stupid?"

"No. I think they just worry."

"My mom worries about everything, but this is the first time Dad's really gotten involved."

"Yeah. I think you're right. Moms worry about everything we do. Dads just worry about us having sex."

"So what does your dad do when you bring a guy home?" I asked.

She shrugged. "It hasn't really happened. I moved up here before I started really dating. I had boyfriends at school, but we just ate lunch together and stuff."

"Does my dad act weird when you have a guy here?"

She thought about it for a minute. "I don't think he's really ever here. Plus, my mom and Ted have a deal. He doesn't interfere with her parenting decisions and she doesn't interfere with his."

"Really? How weird."

With a shrug, she said, "Whatever works." She uncrossed her legs and climbed off the bed. "Let's head downstairs for the night. We'll bring Mojo in early."

I think I was starting to like this having a sister thing.

When I reached the gate to Jonathan's yard, it hit me that I'd never be alone with him again. I knew it was ridiculous to be nostalgic about our time together, but that didn't stop the sentimental yearning.

"What's wrong?" Caroline asked from behind me.

With a shake of my head, I answered, "Nothing." No reason to tell her what a total dork I was.

Buddy and Mojo bounded over immediately, jumping all over us.

I realized we couldn't just grab Mojo and leave. Jonathan would need to know that Buddy was alone out here. Otherwise he'd bark. They'd probably let Buddy in if I took my dog.

"I think we have to knock on the door," I told Caroline and explained the situation.

With one look, Caroline took in my trepidation. "I'll do it. You can just wait with the dogs."

"No. I'll do it. I'll just look like a wimp if I don't." I just hoped his mother wouldn't answer. I didn't know if I could face her after my father had talked to them. No telling what he'd said. I hoped he'd at least omitted the part about holding hands.

"Ally," Caroline said. "You aren't moving. Are you sure?"

"Yes." I started off toward the patio door as fast as I could. Don't think about what Dad may have said. Don't think about Jonathan's mom's reaction. I was so busy talking myself through this encounter that I forgot to watch where I was stepping.

I sank into the grass a little farther than I expected, and when I looked down, I saw my malodorous mistake. I'd stepped into a pile of dog doo.

Caroline, of course, had noticed. She rushed over. "Oh my God, Ally. I'm so sorry." But then she cracked up.

I glared at her, then turned my attention to wiping the bulk of the offensive substance on the grass.

"I know it's not funny, I just can't— " Caroline almost collapsed with her giggles.

I fought the urge to grab her and wipe my shoe on her sandal. Okay, so I did snatch her arm and try to, but she wiggled away to safety.

"You really do have the worst luck," Caroline said from a safe distance. "I've never seen anything like it."

"I prefer to think of it as just having a really bad day," I said. I kept walking around the yard, scraping the dog crap from my shoe. I'd never get it all off, but I was really hoping for most of it.

"Yeah, but it hasn't been that good a month for you either," Caroline started.

"Caro!" I yelled, calling her that for the first time. "Please stop. I don't want to think about it."

I thought I had most of it off now. Ignoring Caroline's laughter...Geez! Would she never stop? I started for the patio again.

The door slid open and Jonathan appeared with his mother close behind.

I guess we'd been making some noise between the laughing and hopping around the yard. My heart skipped a beat. Jonathan looked really good in his jeans. I'd never seen him in jeans before.

Whoever invented jeans deserved my thanks.

"Ally," Jonathan's mother said, drawing my attention from her son's hot bod. "I'm so glad to see you."

"Mrs. Coleman, I'm so sorry."

She interrupted my apology. "Nothing to be sorry about, Ally. I know your father was upset, but Jonathan has explained everything to me. You're welcome here any time."

He has? What exactly had he said? "Thank you," I said to his mother. "I'm glad you aren't angry."

With a wave, she said, "Nothing to be upset about. Mojo is welcome to stay here as long as you need him to. As for the nights, he'll probably be happier inside anyway." Then, she turned to give Caroline an energetic hello. "Would you girls like to come in?"

"I don't know if we should," Caroline said.

Her answer was much better than mine. I said, "I stepped in dog doo." Totally cool, huh.

Jonathan grinned. "When you have a bad day, you really have a bad day."

"Yeah." I couldn't help smiling too. "Sorry about my dad," I told him.

"It's okay," he said. "He just cares about you."

The weird thing was that until a week ago, I hadn't been sure he did care about me. I met Jonathan's warm gaze. "I know."

"Well, I'm going back inside now." His mother motioned to Caroline, "I see you're well chaperoned."

"I think the dog poop will take care of that problem," Caroline quipped.

I sent her a withering glare.

When I turned back to Jonathan, I saw him making a face at Caroline as well.

Something struck me as hilarious, I guess, because I just started giggling. And I couldn't stop. It was probably stress or whatever.

I bent over and put my hands on my knees. I was laughing so hard. When I glanced up, Caroline was looking at me like I was nuts.

"Are you okay?" Jonathan asked.

"Yes," I said. "Great."

"Maybe I should get her home," Caroline said, concern evident in her voice. "I think she's having some sort of breakdown."

"No." I stood up, suddenly much more serious. "I'm okay." It wasn't time for my breakdown yet. I had at least another week or two. Maybe a month. "I'm sorry about my Dad, Jonathan. I hope he wasn't too awful."

Jonathan shook his head. "It's fine. No big deal."

"So what's the scoop, Jonathan? Did you get in trouble?" Caroline obviously had no tact.

"Uh." He shoved his hands in the pockets of his jeans. "No. My parents understood."

"So they didn't research chastity belt on the Internet?" Caroline asked. "Did they make them for boys?"

"Shut up!" I told Caroline. "You are not helping." To Jonathan, I said, "I'm glad things are okay. I guess we should take Mojo and get back before they miss us."

Jonathan's eyes darted toward my house. I just hoped my father hadn't traumatized him.

"Come here, Mojo," Caroline called and held out the leash. She made a big show of hooking it on his collar, as if she were trying to let us know she wasn't watching.

"I should go," I said.

Jonathan took a step toward me. Then he leaned in and gave me a peck on the cheek. "I'll see you tomorrow, Stinky."

I smacked him on the shoulder. "Yeah. Tomorrow."

CHAPTER ELEVEN

Life is just one big pile of dog doo after another, lying in wait in the grass in the backyard. —Ally's Brutal Teen Truths

I stumbled across the lawn towards my stepsister. I couldn't quite comprehend what had happened. He'd kissed me! Like a totally boyfriend to girlfriend casual kind of kiss. In front of Caroline.

"So?" Caroline said as we slipped out the gate.

"I think he might like me."

"Well, duh," she said, like any good sister would.

I know it was lame, but I really didn't want to ever wash that cheek again. I mean, Jonathan's lips had touched it. Without the special middle of the night magic. Maybe he really did like me.

I kicked off my shoes on our patio hoping that offensive substance would disintegrate overnight. We went in the back door, but there really wasn't any sneaking about it. Dad and Diane were sitting on the family room couches waiting for us when we walked in.

"Caroline was with me," I stammered. I didn't do this defensive thing very well.

"We just came down to say goodnight," Diane said. She stepped aside to avoid Mojo while Dad gave him a quick pat on the head.

"We're turning in. We'll be watching television in our room if you need us." My Dad's face hardened as he said, "Don't leave the house."

"What if there's a fire?" Caroline asked in an angelic voice.

"Caro!" Diane warned.

"Just kidding," Caroline called as they went up the stairs.

113

When they were out of sight, she whispered, "You do know what 'watching TV' means?"

Eww. "No, and if you tell me, I'll slit my wrists."

She laughed. "Fine. So did he kiss you? I took forever putting that leash on."

My cheeks flamed with embarrassment.

"He did! Oh, this is so great."

I'd never have any secrets with her around. She could read me better than my mother.

I jumped up on Saturday morning after a truly restful night's sleep. The comfy couch, the temperature control, and Mojo snuggling beside me. Oh, who was I kidding? I'd trade it all in a heartbeat for the hard swing and Jonathan.

Mojo gave me a big lick on the cheek.

"Okay, Mojo. I get it. I'll take you next door."

Caroline was still dead to the world. So I hooked Mojo's leash on and slipped on her slides. They were a size too small. I had hoped to cram my foot in, but it wasn't working. Once the leash made an appearance, I had a limited window to get Mojo outside to a bush without an accident. With a groan, I ran upstairs to get another pair. Mojo followed me, but we were safe. Dad's door was shut. I didn't even want to think about what they were doing last night. Darn that Caroline for putting that image in my head. Watching TV could really mean watching television. Couldn't it?

I grabbed a pair of sandals and we bounded out the front door. Belatedly I thought about my appearance. Hopefully, Jonathan was still asleep. I wanted to see him, but not like this. I probably had eye boogers and a strip of dried drool on my cheek.

I made it back to my house without seeing a soul, which goes to show that my luck isn't always terrible, parental problems and dog doo aside.

I went in the front and headed for the coat closet, the new home of the vacuum cleaner. I picked it up and lugged it down to the family room.

Caroline was still asleep, but I didn't want Diane to come downstairs before I vacuumed. I had sort of promised.

"Caroline," I called in a soft voice. "Are you awake?"
Of course she wasn't, so she didn't answer.
"Caroline, I need to vacuum. Is that okay?"
This time, she responded with a grumble.
Encouraged, I said, "It will just take a minute."
"What are you talking about?" she asked in a grumpy voice. "I'm trying to sleep."
"I just need to vacuum the dog hair up. For your mom."
"Are you crazy? It's barely daylight."
"It's ten," I answered after glancing at the clock. "And I told her I'd do it."
"It's not like it's even necessary."
"What? Of course it is. I gave my word. What do you mean?"
"Nothing," she said too quickly for someone barely awake. She pulled the pillow over her head. "Just do it, already."
I pushed the button and the vacuum roared to life. But Caroline's comment stayed in the back of my mind.
There was only one reason that vacuuming wouldn't be necessary, and that was if Diane's allergies were bogus.
A couple hours later, I worked up the nerve to ask her. "Why'd you say it didn't matter if I vacuumed?"
"Oh," she said, avoiding my eyes. "You know. Because Mom doesn't come downstairs much anyway."
I didn't believe her. But what could I do? Accuse her of lying? Call her mother a bitch? Yeah, I kind of liked that idea, but it wasn't worth ruining our friendship.

Madison and MC came over around noon. We were kind of crammed into my room, which was smaller than my room at home. They were dying to meet Jonathan now that they knew what was going on. So, of course, we headed over to play with the dogs. Jonathan wasn't home. In fact, his house was deserted.
"They probably had a soccer game for Ben," I told them, as I located Mojo's leash and then a second one for Buddy. "Let's go for a walk. One of you can take Buddy."
"Oh," MC said with an exaggerated sigh. "How sweet! You're taking care of each other's children."
"Shut up, MC." God she could be so annoying.

"Since we don't get to meet him, you have to tell us every single detail," Madison ordered.

"I already did," I said as we headed out the gate and down the street.

"No. You only told us the part about sleeping over there and talking and kissing."

"That's all there is."

"We want every single detail," MC commanded. "Spill."

As we pounded down the street in the sunshine, I did. "Okay. So we kind of fell asleep holding hands."

The squealing probably woke people in China.

"Oh my God!" MC said. "This is big."

And Madison started singing off key, "Ally has a boyfriend..."

I just kept walking. I knew I was blushing, and it was silly to be so embarrassed. These were my best friends. But I didn't think I could answer all their questions.

"What did it feel like?"

"Was he a good kisser?"

"Did you wake up and just know it was love?"

They had way more questions than I had answers. The truth was that I was starting to forget exactly what it all felt like. So much had happened in the last twenty-four hours.

MC finally grabbed my arm and slowed the whole parade to a halt. "What did he say last night? Did you get to talk to him?"

I shrugged. "He said my dad wasn't too terrible."

"That's it?" Madison asked.

I looked down at my sneakers. "And he kissed me on the cheek."

More squealing followed. I tugged at the leash and took off in a full run back to the house.

Madison and MC giggled behind me exciting Buddy to enthusiastic barking.

"C'mon Mojo," I said not as winded as I would have been a month ago. "Let's ditch those dorks."

Mojo was happy to oblige.

Later, we were snagging some magazines from Caroline's room when a familiar thudding noise caught my attention.

"What is that?" Madison asked after grabbing the latest Teen People from the top of the pile.

"I think somebody's jumping up and down on your roof," MC said, staring at the ceiling.

With a shake of my head, I said, "No. It's worse. Way worse."

Madison's eyes widened in alarm.

MC narrowed her eyes to tell me she wasn't buying my dramatic act.

"It's," I paused, "Jonathan playing B-ball."

MC squealed. Madison jumped up and down and then headed for the door.

"Wait," I cried.

MC turned back to me. "No way. We are so meeting this guy."

"Please don't embarrass me," I begged as I ran after them.

Hopefully, Jonathan wouldn't mind my friends gaping at him like he was on display at the museum. The long awaited boy who likes Ally. Scientists thought it would never happen...

Jonathan was a good sport. Right? He'd have to be to like me. And I was starting to believe he actually did like me.

I ran down the steps, out the door, and around the corner and almost slammed into MC and Madison. They'd frozen in their tracks. Instead of just Jonathan out there shooting baskets, there were three guys. MC and Madison were regrouping. They wanted to look cool to these new guys more than they wanted to embarrass me.

Dave had noticed our clumsy arrival. From the way he immediately perked up and starting acting even more cocky than usual, I figured he didn't peg us all as losers. "Hey man, we've got company."

Jonathan turned and gave me a big smile that made my heart pitter patter. "Ally!"

Unfortunately, he hadn't realized Colin was taking a shot and the ball bounced off the rim and smashed into his head. His head snapped sideways. He grabbed his head, and then grimaced and socked Colin.

"Sorry, Man," Colin said. He finally noticed MC and Madison.

Jonathan was still wincing with pain, so I decided to do the introductions. "Colin and Dave, these are my friends MC and Madison."

From the way Madison was eyeing Dave, I guessed she had forgotten me telling her about the whole wrinkly Diane breasts incident.

"Do you play?" Colin asked.

"Yes," MC practically shouted before either of us could answer otherwise.

"I'm really not that good," Madison admitted.

If they started simpering and giggling, I was going to kill them. At least Colin and Dave kept them from staring at Jonathan like a bug under a microscope.

"I think I should check on Mojo," I said, mostly because I didn't want to stick around to see what happened next.

Jonathan still had his hand on his head, but he said he'd come with me so fast that I knew he was okay.

As I was opening the gate, I heard Dave saying, "We could play two on two, or we could play horse."

"Let's start with horse," MC said.

Jonathan closed the gate, and I realized we were alone again for the first time in two days. Mojo and Buddy ran up for some attention, but they were apparently worn out from all the company and they walked back over to the patio, slurped up some water, and laid down.

I started to reach out and touch his head but stopped myself. "Is your head okay?"

He nodded. "Yeah. That jerk." He glanced back at the driveway. "Where are your chaperones?"

"I think your hot friends distracted them."

With a grimace, he asked, "You think my friends are hot?"

"No, but MC and Madison do."

His smile returned. "But you don't?"

It took all the guts I had to blurt out, "I think you're hot." The blushing took some of the coolness out of my comment.

Jonathan reached out and grabbed my hand. "I think you're hot too." He said, his voice all low and husky.

I glanced toward my Dad's house to see if Diane had her binoculars or worse, a shotgun trained on us. No sign of anyone.

When I turned back to Jonathan, I discovered that he'd moved a whole lot closer. He took my other hand in his, and leaned forward to kiss me.

My breath caught, and I stretched to reach him.

His lips met mine, and the dizzying sensation of a heated kiss swept through me. He prodded my lips with his velvety tongue, and I opened for him. The next thing I knew, our tongues were tangled in the most amazing dance. He let go of my hands and wrapped them around my back pressing me into him. No one had told me that kissing was like magic. I could feel it sizzling between us. This nameless power. An energy like nothing I'd ever experienced.

The sound of a baby-ish voice broke through the fog.

"Mom, that big, scary man was right. Look! They're kissing!"

Jonathan pulled back and I closed my eyes. I so did not need this.

Jonathan's mother smiled at me when I dared to look. "Ben, that man wasn't scary. He was just upset. He's Ally's father."

"And," Jonathan added quickly, "we weren't kissing, Ben. I was helping Ally, with um, an eyelash in her eye."

His mother beamed. "You see, Ben. They weren't kissing." She winked at us. "Maybe you two better join the others, just in case Ben isn't the only one curious about your...eyelashes."

I could have died right there.

"Thanks, Mom," Jonathan said, and we slipped back through the gate. "Don't worry." He squeezed my hand. "My mom likes you."

I glanced at my friends and wished for the first time in memory that they were not there. "I guess we can try to talk tomorrow," I said.

Jonathan released my hand. "We have to go see my grandmother tomorrow. We'll be gone all day."

If you could go to hell for thinking mean thoughts about someone's grandmother, I was in big trouble.

MC and Madison were giggling as they battled against Jonathan's friends. They must have been playing boys against girls. The girls were obviously getting cremated.

Dave reached around and stole the ball right out of MC's hands.

"I thought they were playing horse," I said to Jonathan.

He shook his head. "I guess they wanted something with more contact."

He was right. Madison had her hands all over Colin as she supposedly went for the ball.

"How come we got busted, and they're out here practically fondling each other in plain sight?"

Dave crashed into MC and sent her sprawling on the front lawn. She was laughing hysterically and he offered his hand to help her up. She refused, and he ended up flailing on the ground next to her. The guys and girls were equally transparent.

Before they could actually jump each other's bones (because honestly, I thought it was coming), Ben made his way out the front door.

"He's like the PDA police," Jonathan mumbled.

"Hey, Man." Colin pointed in Ben's direction. "It's mini-J."

While MC and Madison took in Ben's adorable cuteness, Jonathan explained. "They think he's a mini me."

I glanced from Ben to the hottie at my side. "He does look like you, but I think your friends watch way too much television."

"You have no idea."

Colin overheard us and took offense. "You've seen the whole Scary Movie series twenty times."

Jonathan blushed.

"Yeah, Dude." Dave got up and came over. "You know that because you've watched it with him."

"Those movies are hilarious," MC said.

I gave her a sharp look. She hated those movies. She said they were idiotic.

I turned to see what Madison was thinking, but she was still gushing over Ben.

"Dude," Colin said. "She isn't going to dump you over some dumb movies."

Jonathan squeezed me hand, and I knew he was embarrassed. But I was thrilled. First, I was so not going to dump him. Second, if he was afraid I'd dump him, it meant we were together.

Ben had tired of being left out of the conversation. "Does she got another eyelash?" he asked.

"Uh," I said. I didn't want to bring all that attention down on us.

Jonathan released my hand and swooped down to pick up his brother. "How bout you play a game of horse with us?"

Ben wrinkled his nose at MC and Madison. "Are all those girls gonna play too?"

Jonathan said, "Are you all in?"

"Sure," MC said.

MC and Madison did much better at horse than they had at two-on-two. For one thing, they seemed to actually be trying. Colin and Dave did their best to offer tips, some of which involved touching my friends to show them where to stand. Whatever.

Jonathan rolled his eyes at me. "Oh, Ally," he said with exaggerated gravity. "Let me show you how to do it right."

He came up behind me and wrapped his arms around me. "This will take a while," he said. "I'll have to stand here for about ten minutes hitting on you to do it."

I laughed, not minding the contact or the dig at our friends. MC looked embarrassed and Dave and Colin backed away.

"Not funny, Dude," Colin said.

"Am I interrupting something?" a deep voice asked from behind me.

Jonathan sprang away from me.

Ben backed toward the house.

I turned. "Hi, Dad."

Dad didn't respond. "It's about time you girls went in for dinner, isn't it."

It was not a question.

MC, Madison, and I all dashed for the house.

"Wow," MC said under her breath, "you have the worst luck ever."

Dad didn't say anything to me, and I hoped he wouldn't bring up what he'd seen. After all, there were five other people out there. It wasn't like we were alone. He'd never buy that we were just making fun of my friends.

One problem was solved. No way were MC and Madison going to give me grief after the way they'd acted. They started teasing and I struck right back.

I had a strong suspicion that they had as much trouble getting Colin and Dave out of their heads as I did Jonathan.

"So," MC said after finishing off the pizza. "You take Colin and I'll take Dave."

Madison pretended to think a moment. "Okay."

"You realize they may be sitting next door making other plans."

"Huh?" MC said.

I rolled my eyes. "What if they have the same conversation and Dave picks Madison and Colin picks you?"

MC shrugged. "We're mostly kidding. Do you even know if they have girlfriends?"

"No. I mean, I don't have a clue."

"Call Jonathan's cell," Madison urged. "And ask."

"No way," I said. "Besides, I don't have his number."

"What?" MC's mouth hung open.

"You're kidding," Madison said. "How could you not have his number?"

They were right. I should have his number. "I guess because we saw each other every night, I didn't need it."

MC and Madison shared a look.

"Get it," MC said. "As soon as possible."

Now that I didn't get to see him much, the idea of texting him sounded good. Not as great as spending all night hanging out, but good.

"I was sleeping at his house," I snapped loudly when they did that look again.

They didn't appear convinced. My dad chose that moment to come out of his office. He glanced at me and just shook his head. I was just digging myself in deeper.

When he went upstairs, Madison whispered, "You are like this close to getting homeschooled."

I told them about the chastity belts.

They thought it was hilarious. I didn't. I was starting to think I should buddy up to a locksmith. Or maybe a juvenile delinquent. That guy, Jeff, in Madison's Spanish class was kicked out of public school after he stole the principal's car.

"Do you have to know how to pick a lock to steal a car?" I asked.

"Not if you bash in the window," MC answered.

Darn. I didn't really want Jeff messing around down there anyway. I wondered where the lock was on those things. At the waist, or lower? I shuddered. Ick.

CHAPTER TWELVE

No cute boy will ever really like you. I mean me. Right? And if they do, it so won't last.—Ally's Brutal Teen Truths

My friends left before noon, and I picked up my book, glad for some quiet time. Around two, Caroline stormed the house with Haley and Barb.

"Hey, Ally," Caroline said as she dashed by my room. "Come hang with us."

The thing was that I really didn't want to. "Sure," I called, "Just a sec." I had to go hang out, at least for a while. Just like she had to pretend she wanted me there.

What I really wanted to do was sneak over to Jonathan's house and ask him to run away with me to Tahiti or something. Barring that, I would have loved to just chill and read my book for a while.

Listening to Haley talk about how great she thought she was—so not on my list.

At least Barb had tagged along. With a sigh, I put down my book and went into Caroline's room.

Caroline greeted me with a warm smile. I actually felt like she wanted me there.

"Oh, good," Barb said, "Come sit by me."

I went over and claimed a piece of the bed next to Barb.

"Haley is having a crisis," Barb informed me.

"Oh, sorry," I said. Sorry for myself. Why did I come in here?

"She may have been dumped," Caroline said.

"Caroline!" Haley scolded.

"We aren't sure yet," Barb said.

An hour full of drama queen antics and pouting later, we all decided that she had not, in fact, been dumped.

"Good," Haley said. "Because I'm going to dump his sorry ass tomorrow."

"You just said you're in love with him," Barb reminded her.

Haley tossed her hair. "He's history."

I wasted an hour of my life for this? "I've got to go check on the dogs," I said. "I'll be back."

Caroline nodded. Haley ignored me, and Barb narrowed her eyes. I felt bad for abandoning Barb, but Haley was her friend. There was no reason for me to suffer.

On Monday at practice, I started our scrimmage at center fullback. Things were going pretty well. It helped that I had solid defenders on either side of me.

Then it happened. I was right in front of the goal when Katelyn took a shot. The ball arced right toward me. I started to head it out of the goal. Something stopped me. I knew Amy was right behind me. She was playing goalie, and I didn't like her much, but she was pretty good. I didn't really want to make her mad. The ball flew right over my head and into the goal.

Amy yelled. "You moron! You completely blocked my view of the ball. Why did you duck at the last minute?"

The coach couldn't hear from across the field. "I thought you'd get it," I said kind of helplessly. "You were right behind me."

"If I've got it," she snapped, "then I'll say I've got it. Otherwise, you take it." She turned to Nicole. "I couldn't even see that coming." Then she mumbled a bunch of stuff under her breath.

After celebrating her goal with her team, Katelyn picked up on the tension. "What's the deal?" she asked walking toward us.

"Ally got in my way."

I shrugged. "I thought she had it."

Katelyn turned to Amy. "Yell goalie if you've got it." Then she walked over to me. "If you don't hear her, then go for it. No matter what. And don't put up with her crap. She's a terrible sport."

Katelyn ran back to center field and my team kicked off.

Amy hadn't finished with me though. "You'd better not screw up like that in a game."

I glared at her, and then ran up the field before I could spaz and let them score again.

When practice ended, Katelyn and I ran over to Diane's Range Rover.

"You guys are filthy," Diane said, wrinkling her nose. "I'll put towels down on the seats."

"Uh, Diane, this is Katelyn."

Diane frowned. "I'm sorry dear. I forgot my manners. I'm so glad we worked out this arrangement. I just wasn't thinking about how filthy you two would be."

I stayed back. If she smelled me, she'd never agree to let us in the car.

"Nice to meet you," Katelyn said, shaking her hand. "Thank you for the ride."

We took off our cleats and put them in our soccer bags. That took care of most of the dirt. When we got in the car, Katelyn started to talk about Amy but I shook my head. She got my message. I didn't want Diane in my business.

I jumped in the shower as soon as I got home. I was way too ripe to run into Jonathan. Diane took the towels in and put them in the washer. I thought she was being a little ridiculous.

After my shower, I pulled on clean shorts and a shirt. I knocked on Caroline's door.

"Come in."

"Hey," I said popping my head into her room. "Can you run next door with me?"

She sat on her bed with her laptop. At least ten books were spread around her on the bed. "I hate world history." She got up and slipped on her shoes. "Where's my mother?"

"I don't know."

We went through the house to the front door. Diane was getting in her car. "Hey, girls. I'll be right back. I need to pick up a few things at the store."

We watched her pull out. Then Caroline turned and went back to the house, calling over her shoulder, "She'll be gone for a while. If you need me, I'm in my room."

Walking next door, I really hoped she was right.

I let myself in the fence and played with the dogs. Mojo and Buddy had grown inseparable.

Jonathan slipped out the back and looked around. "No spies?"

I smiled. "Not today. But I have to hurry. Diane ran to the store."

He walked over and petted the dogs. "Did your Dad blow his top?"

"No, he left yesterday morning."

"Alone at last," he said, taking my hand.

"What about," I started to say, stepping back.

Just then, Ben burst out the back door.

Jonathan groaned.

I didn't want to risk forgetting to get his cell number, so I asked for it.

He sort of flinched. "It wouldn't help you any to have it. I can't find my phone anywhere."

"You lost it?" I couldn't comprehend going without a phone.

"Actually," he said, moving closer, "Ben was playing with it last week, and it hasn't surfaced yet."

"Ben lost your phone?"

He raised his finger to his lips. "I don't want Mom to know. She's still mad at us over my iPod."

"He lost your iPod?"

"No. He microwaved my iPod. But I'm hoping he just left the cell phone somewhere in the house."

I looked at Ben with new respect. He could cause quite a bit of trouble for such a small kid.

The little hellion came over and gave me a hug. "Hi, Ally."

"Hi, Ben," I said, squeezing him tight.

"Is that big shouting man really your dad?"

"Uh, yeah." Most people would describe my father as pretty reserved. Until lately. "But he's out of town right now."

"How about giving us a little privacy, Ben," Jonathan said.

His request was met with a confused expression.

"Go play with the dogs so I can kiss her," Jonathan said.

Ben's jaw dropped almost as far as mine.

"Jonathan," I said.

Ben started giggling. "Eeew," he yelled running across the yard. "Gross."

I started laughing so hard I couldn't begin to kiss anybody.

Ben kept screaming. "Eeww! I'm gonna throw up."

Jonathan started cracking up.

The dogs chased Ben, barking as loud as they could.

Then, Jonathan's mother rushed into the backyard to see what was wrong.

Jonathan just shook his head. "I'll walk you home," he said.

His mom shushed Ben.

Jonathan held my hand until we got next door. He walked me to the front door, and gave me a peck on the cheek.

"I'm afraid to risk more," he admitted.

"Good luck finding your cell phone," I said. Pretending to be all cool, I went into the house. Then I waited for him to walk away, and I jumped up and down with excitement. It was starting to sink in. The boy actually liked me.

"What do you mean he lost his cell phone?" MC asked the next day. "How do you lose your cell phone?"

Madison cleared her throat. "Well, you've lost two."

"They were stolen," MC said. "That's different."

I explained about Ben.

MC studied me for a moment as if processing the news. Then she said, "I don't buy it."

Madison and I looked at her like she was nuts.

"What's to buy?" I asked. "His brother lost it."

"If you say so," MC said turning to walk to class.

I sat in classes all day wondering if maybe she was right. Did he just not want me calling? If so, it fit right in with my experience with boys. They never liked me. And with my family experience. Men leave. I wanted to be wrong, but I was growing more stressed by the moment.

I burned off a ton of stress at soccer. I defended Megan's goal instead of Amy's. I really hated playing with Amy. Katelyn told me she'd been playing for years, but that she'd never stayed on one team for very long because nobody liked her. I could totally see why.

Katelyn's mother picked us up. She was really pretty. She dressed like a local news anchor or something. Turned out she was a dental hygienist and only worked part-time.

"I'm so happy to meet you," she said.

"Thanks for agreeing to carpool," I told her. I didn't explain that I wanted to escape my stepmother, but I suspected Katelyn had.

She opened the trunk and had us put our cleats in a plastic bin. Her car had leather seats and a sun roof. I hadn't looked to see what it was, but I wanted one. She didn't freak about dirt, either. Katelyn had been playing for almost ten years. I guess she was used to it.

She pulled up in front of the house to drop me off. Jonathan was shooting baskets in his driveway.

"That's him," I told Katelyn.

She grinned.

I thanked her mom and went next door. I didn't feel like grabbing Caroline to accompany me.

"Hey," he called. His warm smile melted my insides. "How was practice?"

"Good," I said.

"Before you slip away, I wanted to see if you could talk your dad into letting you go to the lock-in on Friday."

My heart thumped. "Friday?" He wanted to spend time with me! The phone thing wasn't a ploy.

"Yeah. Maybe Caroline will go with you."

I'd need somebody to watch Mojo. "Is there a number to call so my dad can check it out?"

"Probably. Just call the Second Pres and ask for the youth minister."

"You're definitely going?" A whole night together. It was almost a date.

"Yes. I always go, but it would be really cool if you could come." His eyes met mine. "We could actually talk."

"I'll do my best." I wanted a kiss, but I was beyond sweaty.

"Go before you get busted. I really want you to come on Friday."

"Good point."

"See you later," he said and turned back to his basketball goal.

I ran for the door. With any luck, I wouldn't get caught talking to him. I could probably talk Diane into the lock-in. Now, if I could get Caroline to watch Mojo.

"No problem," Caroline said a few minutes later. "And I've been to one of those before, so I know Mom will let you go."

My heart swelled with friendship for her. She was really starting to feel like a sister. Sleeping with my stinky dog so I could meet up with a boy.

"You're awesome," I said.

She waved away my compliment. "You'd do it for me. I'll just have to grab him from next door after the football game."

I headed to the shower with a big grin on my face. I was actually going to get to spend time with Jonathan. I guessed he'd probably hang out with his friends some too, but I'd get more than the five seconds alone with him that I was getting now. I could take MC and Madison. They'd love to flirt with Jonathan's friends. And if he blew me off, I'd have back up.

Dad didn't go for it. He asked me a million questions on the phone about who would be there, and why did I want to go to a lock-in at some new church when I didn't even go to the ones at my church.

"Caroline says they're fun. Plus, MC and Madison will be there."

"I'll talk to Diane," he said, "but I'm not happy with this plan of yours."

Diane got Dad to cave. I almost hugged her. She called the church and got the number of chaperones and the planned activities.

I went to bed feeling really confused. Diane had actually done something nice for me. But wasn't I obligated to hate her guts for Mom's sake? The image of her naked flashed through my mind. And the imaginary allergies. Yeah, she had a lot to make up for.

MC and Madison informed me that their mothers had said yes.

"We know you are totally going to ignore us," MC said. "But we're okay with that. Just as long as you find out if Dave and Colin will be there."

"And if they're seeing anybody," Madison added.

It was the least I could do.

Soccer practice on Wednesday was brutal. You'd think the coach wanted us dead, not at the top of our game. I was starting to feel more confident about my abilities. We'd been scrimmaging for an hour each practice, and I'd taken the ball away from some of our best players.

The best part was when Amy was in goal. She didn't call the ball, so I cleared it. Then, she snapped at me again.

"Call it then," I said with all the attitude I could muster.

She sulked, but when the forward shot the ball next time, she yelled, "Goalie!"

I moved and she caught it.

"Much better girls," the coach said from half field. "Now you're working together. Amy, it's the goalie's job to communicate."

I couldn't help smirking.

I didn't run into Jonathan when I got home, so I waited for the sound of his basketball. I never heard that either. MC had called three times. I really needed that information.

Finally, I went next door and got Mojo. I tapped on the back door.

Jonathan came out. "Hey, what's the verdict?"

"I can go," I said. "I'm supposed to find out if Colin and Dave are coming, and if they have girlfriends."

"You can tell MC and Madison that they always come, and neither of them are seeing anyone right now."

"Have they mentioned my friends?"

He shook his head. "They both like all cute girls. I'm sure they'll find time to hang with your friends. A lot of girls will be there though."

Oh. "Is that why you go?"

"No. Just for one girl."

Caroline appeared at the gate. "Mom's looking for you."

"Bye," Jonathan said. "See you soon."

CHAPTER THIRTEEN

Parents are totally unpredictable. No matter how hard you try, you'll never understand them. -Ally's Brutal Teen Truths

Thursday had to be the slowest school day of my life. I was antsy about the game, and I couldn't help thinking about the lock-in. School was really interfering with my schedule. We put on our shiny uniforms, Fighting Irish green, for the first time and hit the field. We were playing a rural public school team that no one expected to be very good. Of course, they didn't expect us to be any good either. The game could go either way.

Coach Borkman told me she was starting me at left fullback. My stomach rebelled, but after a quick trip to the restroom, I decided I might live. Several other girls had hotfooted to the restroom too, so I figured it was normal.

The other team kicked off, and panic rushed through me as the ball headed toward my end of the field. MC was at center halfback, and she was all over the girl with the ball. The girl lost control, and the ball came hurtling toward me. Without any time to think, I got my foot on it and pounded. The ball sailed up the sidelines to Katelyn at left forward. My heart soared. I'd done it, just like at practice. Actually better. Half the time at practice, I kicked the ball out when clearing it.

Ninety minutes later, I walked off the field with an unparalleled feeling of elation. Why had I wasted so many years not playing soccer?

The water in my bottle had gotten warm, but I didn't care. I gulped it down. I'd sweated at least two gallons. I set down my empty bottle and turned to find MC and Madison when I heard my mom calling my name.

Maybe I'd lost too many electrolytes because I knew my mother was nowhere near Charlotte. I swiped at my brow as I caught sight of my mother. She really was there! She ran down the bleachers and hugged me even though I got sweat all over her pristine track suit.

"Oh, Ally. I missed you. I just caught the end, but you were fabulous! I didn't know you could do that!"

"Me either." I pulled out of her hug. "Mom, what are you doing here?"

She wrinkled her nose. "It's a very long story, but the bottom line is that I'm home for good."

"Really?"

"Yes."

"It was a four?" I searched for some sadness in her eyes and didn't find any.

She shook her head. "More like a one point five."

"Sorry," I said.

"I'm not."

MC squealed behind me. "Mrs. Wright!"

Mom waved and MC and Madison mobbed her for hugs. Mom responded enthusiastically despite the sweat rolling off of them.

"I think we all need showers," I said.

Mom laughed.

She dropped me at Dad's and picked up Mojo from next door. Then, she came back for me after I'd grabbed a shower and packed enough stuff to tide me over until the weekend.

When Diane told me goodbye, I just barely resisted saying that it was good I left now before she showed any little sign of allergies.

"Tell me about the one point five." After dropping my stuff in my room and taking Mojo out to pee, I joined Mom on the couch.

Mom rolled her eyes. "It wasn't good. First of all, he never wears pants when he's at home. Just boxers. Even though we'd just met, and he should have been trying to impress me. At least a little."

Ew. I pictured the guy from the Internet in boxers. Luckily, his bottom half was cartoon on the website. I didn't want to picture...Eeeewww!

"Then, I realized that he didn't know anything about his own business. His secretary did all the work. He had to ask her questions about everything."

Mom hated when people didn't stay on top of their jobs.

"And I liked the firm, but I had to work seventy hours a week to keep up. They have a huge caseload, and I had to learn all the local rules. It took much more time than I thought. I started to wonder why I was there to spend time with Donald when I wasn't even seeing Donald."

"Sounds reasonable."

"But the kicker was the gifts."

"He gave you gifts?"

"He gave me all this gawdy gold jewelry which he had custom made. I couldn't refuse it because he couldn't return it, right? It was bad enough that the stuff wasn't tasteful, but then I found out what it really was."

"Huh? What was it?"

Mom had really gotten into the telling and didn't answer my question. "You know how he had that comic book obsession. Well, one day I noticed that one of the comic book characters was wearing a necklace just like the one he'd given me. Let me tell you, that was a creepy realization. So I put all the jewelry in a bag and took it down to the comic book store. The guy identified all of it. The pieces were all jewelry from comic books."

"That's weird."

"Yeah! My spine crawled when he told me. I didn't even discuss it with Donald. I just told him I was leaving and gave the jewelry back. And instead of being upset, he just pulled the jewelry out of the bag and started laying out the pieces to look at." She shivered. "It was disturbing. I'll tell you that."

"Was he crazy?"

"No," she said, shaking her head. "I think he was just weird. In an eerie, unsettling sort of way."

"That's better then," I said, with sarcasm evident in my voice. "Are you disappointed?"

"Not really," she said. "I'd rather find someone right for me who lives on this end of the world." Before I could speak, she said, "And I know you would too."

I laughed. "You do realize that every gift I ever give you from now on is going to be from a comic book."

"That's fine," Mom said, crossing her arms. "And every gift I give you will be as well."

I immediately saw the error of my ways. "Truce?"

"Truce." She put her arm around me and gave my shoulders an affectionate squeeze.

I had my room pretty much set up when my cell rang. "Hello?"

"Hey, Ally. It's me, Jonathan. I found my phone."

Jonathan. I shut my door. Having Mom listen in made me nervous.

"Hey," I answered, trying to sound peppy.

"What the heck!" the deep voice on the other end complained. "I get home late and you've been kidnapped."

"Sorry," I said, glad to hear some distress in his voice. "She surprised me."

"I didn't even get to say goodbye to Mojo."

"We could probably work out some kind of visitation."

He laughed. "We may have to."

"I'm glad my mother came back. But it does suck that we aren't living next door to each other anymore."

He sighed. It warmed my heart. "I guess we wouldn't have seen each other much anyway with your father all ticked off."

"True. Actually, I may be able to see you more with Mom here. Like the other day when your mother invited me in, and my dad said no. My mom would have been cool with it."

"Your mother isn't upset about the, um, situation?"

I shook my head although he couldn't see me. "No, she's not. She gets it." I lowered my voice. "It probably helps that she feels guilty about the whole Mojo adjustment problem."

"Whatever works." I could hear his smile through the phone. "So I'll see you at the lock-in tomorrow."

The lock-in! Oh crap.

"Ally, does that silence mean no?"

"I don't know, Jonathan. I had forgotten about it. I don't want to miss it, but I can't exactly bail on my mother right when she gets home."

He groaned. "We are never going to get to see each other."

"That's not true. I just. I have to think about it."

"The rate things are going we'll have to join the Explorers after all."

"We will if we have to. I'll crawl through the woods with you if it comes to that." *Please, God,* I prayed. *Don't let it come to that.*

Caroline called on my cell soon after. It was the first time she'd ever called me.

"Hey," I said, plopping down on my bed beside Mojo.

"I'm so sorry I missed you, Ally. But I know you're glad your mom is back."

"Yeah. I did miss her."

"So now I don't have to babysit Mojo while you go to the lock-in? Because Liam asked me out for pizza after the game."

"Oh, right. Yeah. I guess you don't need to worry. I probably shouldn't go to the lock in anyway with my mother just getting home."

"You cannot miss it, Ally. It's your chance to spend some time with Jonathan."

"I know, but there will be other chances. Mom wants to go see a movie."

"Did you even tell her?"

"No." She'd had a hard week.

"You should tell her."

"Thanks, Caroline. I appreciate it and all, but I really think it would hurt her feelings."

"I think she should know."

Mom walked in so I lowered my voice. "Thanks for calling, Caroline. And again, I'm sorry I'm missing you cheer tomorrow."

She growled, but said, "Talk to you later, Ally."

Mom has a pensive expression. "Do you want to go to her football game, honey? It's okay if you do."

"No. I'll catch her next week. It's not like it's something that only happens once a year or something." Like the lock in.

Mom came to watch soccer practice on Friday. I thought it was really going above and beyond. I mean, our practices were pretty dull.

MC and Madison were disappointed about the lock-in.

"You guys can still go."

MC shook her head. "Not if you won't be there."

"Plus, we don't even know if Dave or Colin will come." Madison had a point.

Mom let me jump in the shower, and then we headed out to dinner. We were almost to Chili's when she got a call.

A strange call.

"Hello," my mother answered.

Then, she said, "Oh, hi. Uh huh."

After a few minutes of listening, she said, "Yes, dear. Okay, thank you for calling."

"What's up?" I asked after she disconnected.

"I'm not really in the mood for Chili's after all. How about we just run through a Subway?"

Mom was always in the mood for Chili's. "Are you sick or something?"

"No. I'm fine."

"You aren't leaving me again, are you? Was that Donald apologizing for the freaky jewelry?"

"No. You are safe. I promise. Now let's grab some Subway."

I was chewing my sandwich when she said, "I don't think I really want to see a movie. Let's just order something on Pay-per-view."

I nearly choked trying to swallow a half-chewed bite. "Mother, what is wrong with you? Who called? I know something's wrong!"

"Nothing is wrong!" She rolled her eyes. "I wanted to wait until we got home to tell you this, but if you're going to push me...There's been a change of plans for tonight. I'm watching a sappy movie on Pay-per-view, and you are going to that lock-in."

My jaw dropped. "You know about the lock-in? Who called? Madison? Or MC?"

"Actually, it was your stepsister."

"Caroline!" I didn't think Mom had ever spoken to her before. "She called you."

"She was very nice and polite. She just said she thought you shouldn't miss out and she didn't think I'd want you to if I knew what was going on."

I clenched my fist. "I told her—"

"She's right, Ally. I don't want you to miss it. You had these plans, and you should go. I promise, I'll make you my slave tomorrow night. You'll have to let me choose everything we do."

I relented. "If you're sure..."

"Now about this lock-in. I want to talk to someone at the door and verify the number of chaperones."

That sounded more like my mother. "No problem," I said. "It's a church, Mother. They aren't going to host an orgy."

"Allison Margaret Wright!"

"What? I got an A on my report on ancient Greece in sixth grade."

I tried calling Jonathan when I got back home, but he didn't answer. He probably had already left for the lock-in. MC and Madison didn't answer either. I called Caroline.

"You have to go with me now," I informed her. "I'm not going alone!"

"Can't, Ally," she said. "But I'm glad you aren't mad at me. Besides you aren't going alone. You're going with Jonathan."

"I can't get him to answer. He doesn't even know I'm coming."

I could almost see her shrug through the phone. "So, you'll find him when you get there."

"Thanks for nothing," I said.

"Love you too," Caroline said.

I disconnected and found Mom. She had pulled an old sleeping bag out of the closet. "There was a Barbie one in there too, but I figured you didn't want that one."

"Uh, no!"

Mom grinned. "This one should work."

I toted the navy blue, nondescript sleeping bag to the car along with a backpack.

"What's in there?" Mom asked.

"Cell phone, iPod, book for when I'm totally ignored."

"You should probably take some change for soft drinks."

"Good idea," I said. Then I spent the next hour trying on everything I owned.

"How's this?" I asked Mom after I threw on my new sweater and jeans.

"You look great. But aren't you going to be in a hot gym? You don't want to sweat all night."

I was already pulling off my sweater. She was so right.

Finally, I settled on jeans and a cute little top. The bright blue brought out the green in my eyes, and the cut flattered my figure. Well, as much as anything could.

"Perfect," Mom said when I came into the living room.

Mom dropped me at the door of the church's gym. A guy with a clipboard took her name, my name, and an emergency phone number. Then he checked my backpack.

He pointed to the iPod and cell. "These are allowed. Just so you know, they'll probably get stolen."

"It's worth the risk," I said.

Then, he said to my mother, "We don't let them out for any reason. If she gets sick, we'll need you to come get her. You'll have to bring photo ID. Otherwise, she can be picked up in the morning at ten."

Mom nodded. Then, she said to me, "Have fun."

I stalled for a second, tempted to jump back in the car.

The guy waved his clipboard toward the door. "Go on in. There might be some pizza left."

"Thanks," I said. Then I walked into the building, bracing myself.

CHAPTER FOURTEEN

Sometimes you have to take chances, even if you'd rather go play in traffic. -Ally's Brutal Teen Truths

There was a hall outside the gym with various rooms. The noise from the gym indicated that it was the place to be. I peeked in, feeling like a total loser and wishing I knew somebody. A bunch of guys were running up and down the court playing b-ball. I didn't let myself look long enough to determine if Jonathan was there. Instead, I went back out and found a pile of sleeping bags along the wall. I ditched mine with the others, immediately feeling less conspicuous. I walked down the hall and found a kitchen and a game room, both fairly crowded. I didn't recognize a soul.

I found the girls' bathroom and checked out the facilities.

Having stalled as long as possible, I went back to the gym. I entered through the door by the bleachers and sat as quickly as I could. There were a half dozen groups of people scattered around the bleachers. Most of the groups were girls, but there were some guys. A few guys were sitting out but had obviously been playing and were waiting for their turn. Jonathan, who I'd finally located, was among the group of guys running up and down the court. He passed the ball to another guy on the red team and they scored.

It sounded like a herd of elephants with ten guys running at full speed to the other end of the court. Apparently, I should have added ear-plugs to my backpack.

I didn't want to look like some dork drooling over the players, so I started checking out the groups of people. Maybe I'd get lucky and find someone I knew. The only person I spotted was Haley. She was hanging all over some guy, still wearing her cheerleading uniform. A movie with my mother was sounding better and better.

Okay, I told myself. There's no reason to panic. You don't have to go hang with Haley. Just chill like your friends haven't arrived yet. Duh. Why hadn't I thought of that earlier? So I relaxed and watched the game. They were good, of course. I didn't really keep track of the score because I mostly watched Jonathan. I could tell from the intensity that he was "in the zone." He hadn't even noticed me yet. And he probably wouldn't for a long time.

My cell rang and I gave silent thanks. MC was finally returning my call. I didn't bother to greet her. "Thank God, when are you coming?"

"Uh. Ally..."

My stomach clenched. I cupped my hand around the phone so I wouldn't have to shout to be heard over the noise. "No. Don't say you aren't coming."

"I can't. I'm at a movie with my sister. Sorry."

"MC. You have to come."

"Sorry."

Before I could read her the riot act, Madison called in. "Okay," I said. You're off the hook. Madison's on the line."

"But, Ally—."

"Bye." I clicked over. "Hi, Madison."

"Hi, Ally. I just got your message. I'm so glad you got to go!"

"Yeah. Whatever. When are you coming?"

"I can't, Ally. I promised my mother I'd help her plan this bridal shower for my aunt."

"Bridal shower? You don't even know how to plan a wedding shower."

"Of course I don't. But Mom's freaking out about it. She's supposed to meet with her mother-in-law tomorrow. And she's terrified. We're searching the Internet for ideas."

"She's a grown up," I snapped. "She can handle it."

"Oh come on, Ally. You don't need me there. Aren't you hanging with Jonathan?"

"No," I hissed into the phone with a quick look to make sure people weren't listening in. "He's playing basketball. He hasn't seen me yet."

"Well, get his attention."

In this madhouse? "I can't."

"Don't you know anybody?"

"Just Haley, and I'm not hanging out with her. I'd rather go home."

"For heaven's sake."

"If you don't get here in the next half hour, our friendship is over." I used my most firm tone.

She laughed. "Yeah, right. And when Jonathan does see you, I'll be ignored the rest of the night. No. Thank you."

"Thirty minutes," I said and disconnected. I didn't believe for a moment that she'd show up.

In the next ten minutes, some more people came in and sat on the bleachers. I wasn't so obviously alone anymore. Unfortunately, sitting only inches from a group of people at ease with each other only stressed me more.

I decided to take another bathroom break. Unnecessary, but who would know? I climbed down from the bleachers and started for the door, only to hear my name.

I turned to see who knew me. Haley of course.

"Uh, hi," I said. "What's up?"

Haley rolled her eyes. "Caroline called and said for you to come sit with us until Jonathan finishes playing. So what gives? Does he know you're here?"

I blushed. The last person I wanted to look pathetic in front of was Haley. "Uh. No. I was just about to yell to him." MC must have called Caro and begged her to help. How pathetic.

"Really," Haley said, raising an overplucked eyebrow. "Because I can get him for you."

"No thanks. It's good to see you, though. Maybe I'll see you later."

She stuck two fingers in her mouth like she was going to do one of those loud whistle things.

"No!"

She crossed her arms over her chest.

"Fine." I glanced nervously at the court. They were headed back to this end. I had noticed that the guys all looked over at the bench on the other side every now and then. The guys were subbing in and out pretty regularly.

"I'm going to go over there where those guys are and have them pull him out on the next sub." I eyed her. "Is that to your satisfaction?"

She wrinkled her nose. "Lacks drama, but it will do."

I skirted the court to reach the other side and approached the four guys sitting on the bench.

The guy on the end closest to me smiled. "Hey, Ally."

He looked kind of familiar. Oh, Dave. His hair was so wet with sweat that it looked brown instead of blonde.

"Hey, Dave," I said. I sat next to him on the bench.

"Jon said you weren't coming."

"I didn't think I was," I said.

"Has he seen you yet?"

I shook my head. "I thought he'd look over here eventually."

Dave grinned. "Yeah." Then he stood and yelled, "Jonathan," as the guys ran past.

Jonathan tried to glare at Dave and almost tripped. Then, he saw me and grinned.

Jonathan ran over to the bench and another guy rushed into the game.

"Hi," he said. "You came!"

"Yeah, Caroline told my mom and she didn't want me to miss out."

He glanced at Dave and said, "Let's walk a little." I guess he didn't want Dave listening. We walked to the gym door where the hall was surprisingly quiet.

"I'm glad you're here," he said, swiping at his brow with his t-shirt. "I've been playing for like two hours."

"You looked great out there," I said. Then I blushed again.

He grinned. "I've got a change of clothes in my locker. I'm going to head to the shower. If no one's in there making out."

"Okay. I'll be on the bleachers."

"Great," he said, and he jogged off to the boy's room.

Now I was grinning like a fool. I went into the restroom to check my hair. Actually got some lip-gloss out of my backpack. I'd never done that before. I'd also packed a toothbrush and toothpaste because I figured by morning, I'd be really desperate for them.

I only had a few moments with the mirror before a group of four girls invaded. They'd come in to badmouth some other girl.

One of them was all whiny. "Who does she think she is, anyway?"

The others assured her that they didn't know.

"Are you almost done?" One of them asked me. "I'm burning up in there. I need to blot."

I refrained from commenting on her shiny forehead. "Sure." I slipped out the door.

Since I didn't know how long boys took in the shower, I decided to check out the other rooms. The game room was loaded with pinball, foosball, air hockey, and a bunch of guys. The crowd around the pizza had cleared, and only a few kids were in the kitchen grabbing refills on pink lemonade.

I had just finished texting Caroline, MC, and Madison that all was well when Jonathan came up behind me. He smelled like soap and shampoo. "Oh, man. I forgot about the pizza. Is there any left? I'm starved."

"Yeah," I gestured to the counter. "Better hurry though."

He swiped at his damp hair, which had me thinking not so innocent thoughts. It suddenly hit me that he'd really just been in the shower naked. I must be some kind of pervert because that thought sent my pulse racing.

Oblivious to my train of thought, he heaped three pieces on a plate and gave the pink lemonade an uncertain look.

"I've got quarters," I said motioning to the machine in the hall. "Want a coke?"

He set down his plate of pizza and pulled out his wallet. "I've got it. Coke sounds good. Do you want one?"

Before I could even answer, he'd inserted a dollar in the machine and handed me an ice cold Coke. "Yes," I said and waited for him to get another for himself.

He popped his can open, took a long drag, and went back to the kitchen to grab his pizza. "Let's sit out here," he said, leading the way.

I opened my Coke and followed.

He'd found a spot right where the wall curved in that was quiet and almost private. He slid down the wall and sat, already taking a bite of his pizza. "Sorry," he said. "I've been playing for like—"

"Two hours," I finished.

He smiled, fortunately not sharing a full view of the food in his mouth. "So what's up with your mother?"

I told him about the boxers, the comic books, and the jewelry. By the time I finished, he'd inhaled all of his pizza and washed it down with his Coke. He jumped up. "Wait here." Then he rejoined me without the plate and empty can. "Your mother promises never to leave town again?"

"Yes. At least until I'm eighteen. Although she did say that she had a free pass if Mel Gibson called her up." I smirked. "I thought the odds were pretty much in my favor, so I said okay."

Jonathan laughed and took my hand in his. "With your luck, he'll call her."

"Are you saying I have bad luck?"

"Well, you did step in dog doo just the other day. Your dad busted you. And he walked out when I was making fun of our friends, and totally busted us again."

"You made your point. Anyway, I'm thinking of disabling her Internet connection just in case."

Jonathan thought for a minute. "You could report her credit card stolen."

"Or we could hack her profile on the single's sites to make her sound horrid."

"I vote for all three," he said.

"We'll do whatever is necessary," I agreed.

The clipboard guy appeared in the hall and looked around. "Have you seen Kristi?" he asked us. "Short? Blonde?"

We shook our heads.

Another guy came out in green t-shirt that said chaperone. "Find her?"

"No." He tapped the pen against the clipboard.

"I bet she's on the stage again making out with her boyfriend."

The clipboard guy stopped tapping. "She'd better not be," he said. "And next time find a more discreet way to tell me." He angled his head at us.

"Sorry," chaperone guy said and followed him down the hall and through a door.

"Phil's the youth minister," Jonathan said. "He's an okay guy, but these lock-ins always make him uptight."

"Why does he do it, then?"

"To give teens a safe place they can go to stay out of trouble. Didn't you read the brochure?" His brown eyes lit with his smile.

"Must have missed it," I said.

The short, blonde appeared suddenly from the door the others had entered. She stomped down to the middle of the hall and took up her post. Then she scowled at us. "Don't you two have somewhere to be?"

Yikes.

"Let's see if they've started the movies yet," Jonathan suggested.

We went into the third room on the left, which happened to be a nursery with a pretty nice TV. Another green-shirted chaperone was getting the DVD player set up. A few teens had trickled in.

"Let's grab a good spot," Jonathan said. "Did you bring a sleeping bag?"

"It's in the hall."

"Good let's grab those and take a spot against the wall."

I located my bag and turned to find him holding a Bob the Builder sleeping bag. I couldn't help it. I laughed.

He just gave me that crooked smile and raised a brow. "Are you finished yet?"

"No," I said, sucking in some air. The sight of this rugged, athletic guy standing there holding a preschooler's sleeping bag...

"I borrowed Ben's."

"I see that." I finally calmed down enough to follow him back to the room. I could never pull off a sleeping bag like that.

I'd have been humiliated. Jonathan had way more self-confidence than I did.

He got a couple of laughs and remarks as we went to the back wall of the nursery next to two cribs. Jonathan just smiled and said, "You can borrow it next time if you want."

I realized Caroline could have done the same thing. She could bring any embarrassing sleeping bag and pull it off. You just had to have the guts. If only they sold them at the mall. Guts, of course. Not sleeping bags.

"I'm going to buy you a Hannah Montana bag for next time. We'll see how far you're willing to go."

"Bring it on," he said, cracking his knuckles.

"All right guys," chaperone guy said. "Which do want? X-men or We Are Marshall."

After a chorus of disagreement, he said, "We Are Marshall it is."

There were a few grumbles, but he put in the DVD and dimmed the lights.

Jonathan leaned back against the sleeping bags and motioned for me to join him. He took my hand in his. I'd never realized a church nursery could be so romantic.

"And no making out," chaperone guy said with a look in our direction.

Giggles followed, and the guy sat down to watch the movie. Okay, maybe not.

Jonathan put his arm around me, and I scooted a little bit closer. Not making out, but still heaven.

I was so glad my mother didn't let me miss this. And Caroline. I'd have to really thank her too.

Jonathan leaned close to my ear, and I could feel his warm breath as he whispered, "Did I mention that I'm glad you got to come?"

"Yes," I whispered. "Me too."

Then, he gave me quick little kiss next to my ear and turned back to the movie.

By the time the movie ended, my butt was asleep. I didn't care. It was totally worth it. Not the movie, but cuddling with Jonathan.

The lights came on and we all blinked.

"What next?" Jonathan asked.

"You can go back and play b-ball with your friends if you want," I said, just to be nice.

He shook his head. "Thanks, but no. They've probably all collapsed from dehydration by now."

The chaperone guy went over to the television. "Our second half of the double feature will be X-men."

"I can't feel my legs," I admitted to Jonathan.

He grinned and stood. Then he pulled me to my feet. "Is that better?"

"Not yet."

He stood patiently waiting for blood to find its way back into my feet.

"Okay," I said finally. "I'm good."

We went out into the hall. Most of the movie watchers had tired of the nursery, but new people were coming in as they heard X-men was about to start.

"Where are we going?"

"I'm not sure," Jonathan admitted. "Apparently the stage is off limits."

"And under patrol."

We peeked in the gym. The guys had stopped playing basketball. A group of girls was dancing in one corner. They weren't very good at it. One of them, a chubby blonde, appeared to be teaching the others some moves. I cringed in sympathy.

The smell of old socks hung in the air, and I was glad Jonathan had taken a shower. Oh no. There were those impure thoughts again. Luckily we had enough outside influences to tone down the Catholic guilt about having normal teenage feelings.

"I've got an idea." He headed to the bottled water machine. "This is Phil's office." Just past the office, on the other side of the machine, were two empty chairs. My backside much appreciated the idea of a real chair. "I was hoping nobody would be over here. It's too close to the office."

He turned the chairs so that they faced each other and we'd be pretty well hidden by the machine. We sat and he lifted my hand and kissed it. I could have melted right there.

The sound of hushed voices and rapid footsteps approached.

Then Clipboard Guy's voice was saying, "We've got all the parents coming except for Haley's. We need to try her house again."

One of his minions said, "What were they thinking playing strip poker at a church?"

Clipboard Guy said, "Some teenagers just don't think. They don't learn to think until they're twenty."

"Hey," the other guy replied. He apparently wasn't twenty yet.

"I said some," Clipboard Guy grumbled as they went to his office.

When they were clear of us, I gave Jonathan a wide-eyed look. "Haley was busted for strip poker!" I whispered excitedly.

Jonathan's mouth quirked into a grin, and we both covered our mouths, quaking with laughter.

Haley completely deserved it.

The voices from the office reached us again. "Go check in with Tina. And try to find those two couples from the movie room who were so cuddly. I don't want them slipping away without our noticing."

I stopped laughing.

Jonathan's eyes lit with mischief. He pointed to himself and then to me.

Not only was I part of a couple, but I was on the radar screen for demonstrating affection. My life had changed a lot in the last two weeks.

The footsteps moved farther down the hall.

I gave Jonathan what felt like a saucy grin even though I didn't know I had that in me.

He put his arms on my shoulder, gently pulled me close, and touched his lips to mine.

Oh. My. God. A strange hunger swept through me as he deepened the kiss. Tenderness gave way to desperate ferocity, and his hands came around my back to pull me to him. I went willingly, sliding forward and threading my hands through his damp hair. I forgot about the water machine and the chaperones and the gym full of people. It was just me and Jonathan and his powerful kiss.

A frustrated, "Oh for crying out loud," brought me back to reality.

A chaperone stood glaring at us with arms crossed. "Cut it out. We've got enough crap to deal with tonight."

"Sorry," I whispered trying to clear my head by blinking a few times.

"Look," the guy said. "Get to the gym and I won't say anything to Phil. He's already up to his armpits in trouble."

Jonathan had the presence of mind to mumble a thank you.

The guy gave us one last look before going into the office.

Jonathan took my hand and we ran down the hall to the gym, giggling. Well, I giggled. He just trembled with laughter.

"At least they didn't kick us out," I said.

"Luckily we aren't their biggest worry." He stopped inside the gym door. "Want to go watch X-men?"

"Yeah," I said.

Two hours later, we dragged our sleeping bags into the hall. Chaos still reigned in the gym, but they'd designated the hall for sleeping. Two chaperones watched like hawks from either end.

We lay side by side, talking softly. Jonathan was telling me about Dave and Colin's antics. They sounded a little crazy, and I could totally see my friends hooking up with them.

"Can you spend the night with Caroline every once in a while?" Jonathan asked.

"Sure. They'll watch me though."

"That's okay," he said. "We can just hang or play ball or something. We don't have to spend all our time making out."

I snorted. "We don't?"

"Well," he said with a sigh. "In a perfect world..."

Eventually, clipboard guy came by and said, "Sleeping bags two feet apart."

I scooted and he scooted and we managed the required space.

Clipboard guy nodded and walked down the hall to someone else.

Jonathan reached out and found my hand. "I liked the dogs better."

I just smiled.

ABOUT THE AUTHOR

Juli Alexander writes young adult romances and paranormal young adult fiction. *The Karma Beat* will be followed by the sequel—*The Techno Echo*—in early 2013. Check out *Stirring Up Trouble* and the sequel—*Trouble's Brewing*. *Stirring Up Trouble* and *Valentine's Day Sucks* are available now at all retailers. *Trouble's Brewing* will be released summer 2012. Don't forget to check out the YA anthology, *Eternal Spring*, featuring "Camp Cauldron" by Juli Alexander.

Juli's house is overrun with dogs, dirty laundry, and teenage boys. writing keeps her relatively sane. You can find her at julialexanderauthor.com or on twitter @juli_alexander.